STONE DEEP

MICAH REED BOOK 5

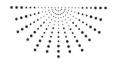

JIM HESKETT

OFFER

Want to get the Micah Reed novel **Airbag Scars** for FREE? It's not available for sale **anywhere**. Check out www.jimheskett.com/free
for this free, full-length thriller.

And read on after the main text for some fun, behind-the-scenes extras.

Gonna climb the road to heaven
    Down by the riverside
    I ain't gonna study war no more
    Study war no more
    Ain't gonna study war no more

— TRADITIONAL

PART I

THE BORN-AGAIN VIRGIN

A GLOVED FIST whiffed through the air, and Micah Reed managed to lean his head far enough to the left that he didn't lose any teeth when the punch connected with his jaw. His boxing partner Layne Parrish was a beast of a man. Tall, muscular, covered in faded and fleshy tattoos. Micah wasn't tall, or buff, or decorated with ink. He used to fancy himself an above-average boxer, but Layne's ass-whooping was teaching him otherwise.

The most recent blow nearly sent Micah to the mat, but he was able to save a little bit of dignity by skidding into the ropes instead. The ropes wanted to catapult him back to the middle of the ring, but he wrapped a glove around the top rope to stay in place.

He held up his free hand and spit out the mouth guard. "Uncle. I'm waving the white flag. I think you've kicked my ass enough for today."

Layne cackled and shadow-boxed the air between them. "Sure, man, if you say so."

Micah caught his breath as Layne lifted the ropes for him to exit the ring, and both of them thudded onto stools to remove their gloves. Micah's heart raced so fast he had to pause for a minute first. Around them, Glazer's Gym rumbled with movement, sound, and the stink of sweat. Micah loved this place. It was close to his home in downtown Denver, was funky, run-down, and anonymous.

Micah appreciated anonymity. Not only because Micah wasn't actually his name, but also because sometimes, you want to be one among many. To blend into a place where nobody knows your name, and nobody would care to know it.

"Got plans tonight?" Micah said.

Layne sipped from his water bottle and splashed some on his head before answering. "Not really. Going to see my daughter tomorrow, then I'm out of town for work for a couple weeks. You're not interested in dogsitting my Bullmastiff while I'm gone, are you?"

"Nope. Not even a little bit. Sorry, Layne."

"No big deal. You got plans?"

"Frank's got me doing some research at the office. Stuff I should have done already. But what can I say? I slacked off, and now I'm paying the price."

They stood and then navigated the dirty floor to return to the locker room. After hitting the showers, they walked out together, chatting about travel plans for

Christmas and New Year's Eve. Micah had none, of course. No family trips on the horizon since most of his immediate family thought he was dead. And, being four-teen months sober in AA, he didn't see the point in going out for a big New Year's bash.

Outside, Micah cinched his coat close as snow trickled from the sky like white confetti in a parade. Layne, wearing only a long sleeve t-shirt, grinned at Micah's heavy coat.

"I seriously don't get how you can't feel cold," Micah said.

"Oh, I can feel it, man, I just don't care."

Micah was about to reply when Layne held up a hand, pointing at a man standing next to Micah's car, across the lot.

"You know that guy?"

Micah focused his eyes, then identified a white man with dark hair standing next to Micah's beat-up Honda Accord. Blue suit, wool coat and scarf around his neck. Arms crossed, a leather messenger bag hanging across his body.

Gavin Belmont, US Marshal.

"Yeah," Micah said, grimacing, "I know the guy."

Layne cracked his knuckles and stepped closer to Micah, while eyeing Gavin. "You don't seem happy to see him. Everything okay?"

"It's fine. I think I should probably talk to him, so maybe I'll catch up with you later?"

"Sure, man. Hit me up if you need anything."

Micah endured Layne's punishing grip to shake his hand, and then waited until he'd left the area before approaching Gavin. Without speaking, Gavin tilted his head at the car and walked around to the passenger side.

Micah slid in and unlocked the door for the Marshal.

"Hi, Gavin," he said as his former handler had a seat and unraveled his scarf. "We've got to stop meeting like this."

Gavin approximated a smile. "Feels like yesterday, doesn't it?"

"What do you want, Gavin?"

"There you are again, with that attitude. I thought after everything that happened last time, we'd gotten past all this. I thought we'd come to an understanding."

Micah bit his lip. "You show up unannounced, inserting yourself into my life whenever you see fit. I told you before, this is one of the reasons why I dropped out of the program. I don't want to live like this anymore. I want my autonomy back."

Gavin sighed, and Micah felt a pang of guilt. He didn't know why he persisted in being so resentful toward this man who was only a few years his senior. Objectively, the Marshal wasn't a bad guy. But Micah still felt an irresistible urge to punch this man in his stupid face.

"Odd choice for a gym," Gavin said.

"How so?"

Gavin pointed behind him. "It's right down the street

from the Pink Door. You know who owns the Pink Door, right?"

"I do know, and I don't care. Tyson Darby hasn't hassled me in a long time, so I don't consider it to be a problem. What do you want, Gavin?"

"Okay, I'll get to the point, if you're not in the mood for small talk." He opened the messenger bag and removed a folder. From inside that, he handed Micah a black and white photograph of some guy with brown skin, messy black hair, and a tattoo of a skull on his neck. Looked about Micah's same age, late twenties or early thirties.

"Should I know who this is?" Micah said.

"I doubt it. His name is Santiago Jiménez, but he goes by Snoop. Former cartel."

"Sinaloa?"

"No," Gavin said, "not one of your old crew. He was with an outfit named Dos Cruces, out of Baja and Southern California. Ever heard of them?"

"Yeah, I know Dos Cruces. They stayed far enough away from us that they weren't a problem. The Sinaloa never had any beef with them, as far as I know."

"Good. That's helpful."

"Why are you showing me a picture of this Snoop guy?"

Gavin went back to the folder and withdrew a few more pictures. He plopped them into Micah's hands. When Micah looked down, the pic on top nearly turned his stomach. A row of corpses, partially-covered with stained sheets. Many of the corpses' limbs were exposed. Bubbling skin, bulging eyes, tongues lolling out.

After only a second or two, Micah had to look away. His stomach scrambled like two alley cats fighting.

"What the hell, Gavin? What is this?"

"The literal name is N5A9, but few people know it by that name. It's sort of like a strain of smallpox, but it's much more sinister, as you can see."

There were three more pictures underneath the one on top, but Micah didn't page through them. He dropped the stack on top of the Honda's center console and folded his hands. "Please don't surprise me like that again."

"Sorry."

"You said you were going to get to the point."

Gavin cleared his throat. "Santiago Jiménez, during his time in the cartel, stole some of this smallpox strain from a group of particularly nasty Serbians to give to Dos Cruces. It's never been recovered."

"And?"

"And we need to recover it."

"So, why don't you pick him up, sweat him, throw him in jail? Isn't that what you people do best?"

Gavin shook his head. "FBI and others have tried that several times. Claims he doesn't have it, and he's been on-message about it since we first questioned him. If he does know where it is, he's not telling. Believe me, we've used every method of interrogation, turned over every rock." Gavin reached back into the bag for a different folder and pulled out a printout.

Micah glanced at it, hesitantly, not wanting to witness any more real life gore. But the image seemed tame. A building for sale, some old abandoned mall. "And this is?"

"That's a piece of property for sale in Las Vegas. Actually, not for sale anymore. It's sold now. There's a Nevada billionaire—I'm not going to tell you his name, but he's previously been under investigation by the FBI—who's selling it."

Micah felt a little itch under his skin. He had a connection to Las Vegas, but he didn't know if Gavin knew that. "And?"

Gavin set another picture on top of the printout. Two men in suits, shaking hands. The one on the left looked familiar, and when Micah saw it, he gritted his teeth. Kellen McBriar, Micah's older brother. Micah hadn't seen him in five years, maybe six. Not since before everything happened and Micah had disappeared. Before anonymity.

"That's my brother Kellen."

"Is it coming together yet?"

"What does my brother have to do with this crooked rich guy?"

"That's a photo of your brother shaking hands with the billionaire I mentioned. They're newly-minted partners. Kellen just entered into a deal to buy that piece of land, and he's going to lose everything. It's a rotten deal."

Micah stared for a few seconds, letting the information sink in.

"Now," Gavin said, "you might be thinking, since your living situation prevents you from contacting your brother yourself, that you're going to call someone and get a message to him. To tell him not to do the deal. Well, it's too late for that. Paperwork has been signed. It's already in the bag."

Micah's shoulders tensed. He didn't like where this was heading because he knew Gavin was gearing up to turn this into a sales pitch. "Okay."

"But, it's not too late for us to get him out of it. I have authority from the Justice Department to scrub your brother clean of this business arrangement so he doesn't lose his life savings. It won't be easy, but it's possible."

Micah stared at the grainy black and white picture of Kellen McBriar. He couldn't see enough detail in the photo to detect if Kellen had wrinkles around his eyes, but he spotted a healthy amount of gray running through Kellen's dark brown hair. Kellen was four years older, which would make him thirty-four? Thirty-five? Micah had known his brother was living in Vegas, doing well for himself, but not much else. Whatever he could glean from Kellen's public social media posts. Wife, two kids, a few business ventures out in the desert.

Seeing this picture of his big brother tugged at Micah's loneliness. His isolation from his family. And Micah resented that Gavin would have known that. Gavin could help Micah's brother, but obviously, there had to be a price. Micah dropped all the pictures except for the one of Santiago Jiménez, AKA Snoop.

"And it has something to do with this guy and his smallpox strain. What do I have to do to get you to scratch my back?"

Gavin nodded. "We want you to get close to Snoop. Undercover, in a sense."

"Undercover. Can I be a British person? I've always wanted to try the accent."

Gavin frowned. "This isn't anything to joke about."

"I've got to deflate the tension somehow after you blitzed me with those disgusting pictures, don't I?"

"Again, I'm sorry about that. I thought you needed to see it, to understand how grave this is."

"Yeah, Gavin, I get it. What is it you want me to do?"

"Find out if he still has the smallpox and where he's keeping it. We think he's about to do a deal to offload it."

"Why do you think that?"

"Because 28 days from now, he's on a plane out of Tulsa to Vietnam, to move to a halfway house there. Vietnam has no extradition treaty with the US. We will likely never see him again."

"Halfway house?"

Gavin reached into the messenger bag yet again and produced a pamphlet for *Cornerstone*, a treatment center in Perkins, Oklahoma. He dropped it in Micah's lap. Micah paged through the pamphlet, eyeing pictures of some spacious mansion set among rolling hills and a vast expanse of wooded greens.

"Snoop checked into treatment at Cornerstone today. Locals call it The Stone. We think he's going to make a deal while he's there. This is a perfect situation, Micah. You have experience with drug and alcohol recovery. You're from Oklahoma. You have cartel experience. There's no one in the world more qualified to work this guy."

"I have things to do here in Denver," Micah said. "I have a job, you know."

"It's all cleared with Frank. He's going to be working with me for the next 28 days while we explore some alternate angles."

"And if I don't do this, you won't help my brother."

Gavin frowned. "Don't treat it like extortion or blackmail. Your brother got himself into this mess. The Marshals and the FBI are willing to take this risk for Kellen because recovering this smallpox strain is so critical."

Micah rolled the Cornerstone pamphlet into a tube as he gritted his teeth. Felt manipulated. Once again, he was under the thumb of the feds, with no choice but to do their bidding. But, if he refused, Kellen would suffer. Would lose everything. Micah had done enough damage to the McBriar family already, and he couldn't imagine being responsible for more.

Not to mention this smallpox strain. Those ghastly pictures of the corpses were a strong selling point.

"I'll get you fully briefed today," Gavin said, "and then

you'll be on a plane tonight. 28 days, Micah. We're on the clock here."

Micah stared at the picture of his brother shaking hands with a man who would steal his life savings. Probably his kids' college funds. Micah knew he had to do this.

And he also knew the Marshal wasn't telling him the whole story.

"Fine, Gavin. I'll do it."

DAY 2

MICAH DROVE THE rental car down Smith Street in Perkins as the monstrous mansion of Cornerstone Drug and Alcohol Treatment Center loomed ahead. Gavin had given Micah the crash course briefing yesterday. Some former oil baron had donated the building thirty or forty years back, and they'd constructed dorms for housing behind it. The mansion sat at the near end of a hundred acres of pasture, filled with basketball courts, meditation gardens, endless forests teeming with pecan trees.

Micah hadn't gotten sober at a posh place like this one. Fourteen months ago, he'd sweated out his last drink at a ratty detox in Denver, after several failed attempts during his first year living in Colorado. His first year as Micah Reed, brand new person, brand new social security card. Anonymity. Before that, prison, and before that, working for the Sinaloa cartel until the feds had barged into his life and turned everything upside down.

Micah parked at the edge of the gravel lot and gazed at the tan brick building. Three stories, and at least eight or ten thousand square feet. Like a fortress or castle, but without the arrow slits and cauldrons of boiling oil.

"Holy shit, Boba, look at this place," Micah said as he fingered the severed head of a Boba Fett action figure, sitting in his pocket. Micah's constant companion since High School.

Boba Fett said nothing.

Micah had 28 days to learn about this Snoop person and to earn his trust. 28 days until a chance to recover this smallpox strain disappeared down the drain and Snoop would escape to the other side of the world. And Micah's brother would suffer for it.

Once again, Micah was going to have to pretend to be someone else. A person on his first day of sobriety, sifting through the ashes of a drunken existence. At least Micah had lived through that once before, in real life.

He left the rental and weaved through the cars in the lot until he came upon a young man sitting on the steps, smoking, suitcases around him. The kid couldn't have been more than twenty. Sour look on his face.

"Checking in?" the kid said.

Micah nodded. "Checking out?"

The kid flicked his cigarette down the steps and exhaled a cone of acrid smoke in the chilly morning air.

"Not by choice, bro. I know it looks like a castle, but trust me, it's more like a dungeon."

Micah wanted to roll his eyes, but resisted the urge. Kids could be so dramatic. "What does that mean?"

"Mess up once, they put you on Contract. Mess up again, and you're done. No third strike, no touchy-feely, come-to-Jesus sit down with your counselor, no nothing."

"How did you get on Contract?"

"Caught me in a chick's room after curfew."

"And what about after that?"

The kid lit a fresh cigarette. "Caught me doing the same thing last night."

Micah wanted to say, *well, it's not like you didn't know the rules*, but that wouldn't mean anything this kid. Like any addict, he would put the blame squarely on the shoulders of everyone else in the world. Micah knew this phenomenon well.

"That sucks," Micah said.

"Hell yeah, it does. I broke my court order. I'll have to do a few months in jail unless my lawyer can work some magic. Can I give you a piece of advice?"

"You can try, but I'm pretty full-up on advice."

The kid pointed a finger at Micah. "I don't know if you're here because of a judge, or your wife and kids, or if you're here for real. But only about half the people who enter actually graduate. That's a fact. And even if you do make it through to the end, there's no guarantee you'll stay sober." The kid tilted his head back at the mansion. "I was sixteen, my first time through here. The Stone stays the same, but I get worse each time."

The gravel behind Micah crunched, and the kid flicked his cigarette, stood, and grabbed his bags. "Good luck," he said, and then stomped down the stairs, toward the car waiting for him.

~

The nurse checking Micah in was a Native American named Oscar, towering and thick, with long hair like strings of seaweed. Big, distracting warts on his face. Maybe he looked like a witch, but Oscar had a kind smile and watery brown eyes. For someone who likely spent the majority of his days with surly and still-vibrating drunks, he had an air of patience about him.

"Mr. Templeton," Oscar said, and for a second, Micah didn't lift his head. The pseudonym felt foreign.

"Yes," Micah said.

They were sitting at a desk in the hallway leading out to the lobby, some sort of check-in station, filling out paperwork. Micah had been distracted by the opulence of the interior. Marble everywhere, glittering chandeliers, ornate frescoes carved into the ceiling. This was nothing like the run-down detox where he'd gotten sober.

Oscar lowered his head and caught Micah's eye. "Are you okay? Would you like some orange juice?"

Micah had to remember he was supposed to be only

one day free of alcohol. He tried to recall how that felt. Physically ill, nervous, shaky. Paranoid about everything and everyone. Always waiting for the hammer to descend.

He shook his head. "No thanks. I just want to get this paperwork over with, to be honest. I'm ready to rest."

Oscar nodded, and they continued with the forms. Most of the info had been planted already by Gavin's people. Micah Templeton, treatment paid for by a private donor. Full 28-day stay. All of it arranged so Micah didn't have to fill in too many blanks or remember too much backstory.

Being here, at this treatment center, was a surreal experience for Micah. So much about it was familiar, yet not. The men and women wandering through the lobby and hallway were alcoholics and drug addicts, but not all of them were here for honest reasons. Many of them would have been court-ordered. They would wait until their time was up and then deliberately return to their drug lives.

Micah had returned to his home state again after entering—and subsequently dropping out of—Witness Protection. Ten miles down the road from here was Micah's old apartment in Stillwater. A place where he had consumed many thousands of beer bottles, had spent countless lonely nights feeling sorry for himself. A place where he tried not to bring home the horrors of his day job, although he rarely succeeded at that.

Only ten miles down the road. But he had no desire

to visit his old stomping grounds.

28 days to get the info out of Snoop Jiménez, rescue his brother's life savings, then Micah would be gone and back to Denver.

Oscar's questions were all about Micah's drinking history, and Micah mostly told the truth about that, except for the fact that he hadn't had a drink in fourteen months. He fudged the timeline, but the rest was accurate.

"Do you drink in the mornings?" Oscar said.

"Sure, but only on special occasions, like Tuesdays."

Oscar didn't laugh at the joke.

The nurse got Micah to fake-admit that he drank to help him go to sleep at night. That he sneaked drinks when he was around coworkers and family. That he felt ashamed of his secrets.

After the paperwork, Oscar led Micah to what they called the "recovery suite," which was a fancy name for the detox wing of Cornerstone. It was room to the side of the nurses' station, away from the rest of the treatment center. Micah would have to spend his first three days here before he'd be allowed to mix with the regular treatment people.

Just like protective custody in prison.

There were four of these suites, two for men and two for women, clustered together. Micah wondered if Snoop was in the other male suite, because there was an occupant already in the room, and that man was not Snoop Jiménez.

The guy sitting on the opposite bed had dark skin, was short and skinny, with curly black hair and a wispy mustache. A cowboy hat rested on the nightstand next to his bed.

"Morning," the guy said. "I'm Nash."

Micah crossed the room and extended a hand to shake. "Micah."

Micah realized he'd been a little too eager, but Nash didn't shy away. When Nash lifted his arm to shake, Micah gazed down at a series of white scars up and down Nash's forearm. Like slugs.

Nash noticed him noticing, and smiled. "I'm not a cutter, if that's what you're thinking."

"I didn't…"

Nash shook his head. "That was a bull in El Paso." Nash extended his left leg and rolled up his sweatpants, revealing a scarred-up knee. "Ended my career, that son of a bitch."

"Rodeo?"

"Youngest black triple-crown winner in US history. As a matter of fact, maybe the *only* black triple crown winner in history. The brothers don't go much for roping and riding."

Micah dropped his bag on the bed across the room and sat next to it.

"Here's the part," Nash said, "where you tell me about your one black friend. Where you try to get me to understand that you're one of the good ones."

Micah had a notion of what was coming next, so he

kept his mouth shut and waited for Nash to continue.

"You got one black friend, right?"

"Actually, I do. He's my boss, Frank."

Nash tilted his head, looking impressed. "Boss, huh? That's a step in the right direction."

Micah got the feeling that, at this moment, anything he said would be the wrong thing. Like any drunk, Nash seemed moody and quick-tempered. So, Micah kept his mouth shut.

Nash held the silence for a few seconds, then he laughed, but it felt forced and weird. "I'm just messing with you. You can hang with whoever you want. Ain't none of mine."

"Thanks," Micah said.

"Whatever you did out there, it don't mean a fuck in The Stone."

Nash shuddered and reached for a juice box on the nightstand. As he lifted the drink to his lips, the straw jittered. Micah flashed back to being in detox, wallowing among other sick people, many of them sullen and prone to outbursts.

"First week," Nash said, "everybody brags, *man, I used to do so much drugs.* Second week, everybody says, *I can't believe I used to do so much drugs.* Then, third week, they're all saying, *please, do not talk about drugs anymore.*"

Nash cackled to himself and sipped his juice.

"You sound like you know your way around this place," Micah said.

"That I do, Micah. It may look pretty, but it's filled

with some of the most sick and suffering bastards you'll ever see. People don't fly in here on the wings of victory, if you get what I'm saying."

The reality of the situation was beginning to sink in. Micah was stuck here for 28 days, isolated and alone among a crowd of drunks and druggies who also felt isolated and alone. Plus, something about this Nash character struck Micah as wrong. Maybe because Nash was detoxing, which added a sheen of unease to everyone.

"I think I know what you're saying," Micah said.

Nash nodded. "What are you in for?"

"Alcohol."

Nash pointed at his knee. "Painkillers. You been to The Stone before?"

Micah shook his head.

Nash opened the nightstand and took out a can of chewing tobacco, and inserted a plug of the brown stuff into his mouth. He chuckled, a booming and sustained sound. "A virgin, eh? This'll be my third trip through here. Gonna do it different this time, though. Gonna actually follow through with my relapse prevention plan. Gonna be a whole new person when I walk out of here."

Micah hoped for the same thing, for entirely different reasons. He was already sober. But, if he succeeded here, he could not only stop a bad man from doing bad things, he could keep a good man from losing his life savings. But, Micah couldn't say any of that to Nash.

"Yeah," Micah said instead, "me too."

DAY 5.1

MICAH SPENT HIS three days in detox keeping his head down and trying to glimpse his target Snoop. He didn't get much of a chance. Oscar and the other nurses watched him and new roommate Nash closely. Kept them quarantined like contagious people. Coming in every two hours to check their vitals, deliver their meals, and talk to them about how they were feeling.

A long, slow, boring three days.

Since phones and computers weren't allowed in treatment, Micah had spent his free time catching up on sleep and reading some terrible thriller novel that had been left in the room. Cheesy plot, awful dialogue, unrealistic plot twists. But, the dog-eared paperback was all Micah had, so he read it cover to cover. Turned out, the wife had been the one plotting the husband's death the whole time. Surprise, surprise.

In the middle of the night on the second day, Nash had started babbling in his sleep. Micah crossed the room and hovered next to the bed as Nash, sweating and shaking, grumbled and roared like a dog barking in its sleep.

Micah reached out to touch his roommate, and Nash responded by smacking Micah's hand away.

Nash sat up, horrified. "What are you doing?"

"You had a bad dream."

"And you're just going to stand over me like some stalker? Seriously, that's not cool."

"No. I didn't. I'm sorry, Nash."

Nash glowered at him, and Micah wondered if being nice was the wrong way to go with this guy. Nash had proven to be temperamental and hard to predict. Maybe Micah needed to play tough to earn his respect.

Either way, it didn't matter, because a moment later, the lights blinked on and the nurses rushed in to take Nash's vitals.

After that, there were no more nightmares, and Nash and Micah sometimes went hours without speaking. Other times, Nash would regale Micah with tales from the rodeo. Micah assumed at least half of them were fabricated. You can always count on newly-recovering drunks to lie their asses off if they think it will impress you or make you like and/or fear them. Micah said little, but he did tell Nash the true story of his last drink. The night of his trip to the Pink Door strip club, blacking out and crashing his car into a ditch off Highway 287.

Except, in the new version Micah told, the story had happened a week ago, instead of more than a year ago.

After three days in the recovery suite, they finally let Micah and Nash out to mix with the rest of the treatment center population. Micah's first mission had to be to hunt down a phone to check in with Frank. He wandered through the Cornerstone lobby to a room that looked like a library, with a few people lounging on couches.

Micah stopped for a moment to stare out the window. Two young men were sitting in the frozen grass beside a basketball court, playing guitars and singing.

He flashed back to being twenty years old, to an argument he'd had with his brother when they were both at their parents' house over mid-semester break. Micah had picked a fight with Kellen over something silly; something his brother had said at dinner. Micah couldn't even remember the topic now.

Kellen was in grad school, and Micah was on academic probation at Oklahoma State. About to flunk out. Micah had been jealous. He hadn't realized it at the time, of course. He'd only known he was angry at his brother. One of many times Micah had been unreasonable and Kellen had been forced to play peacekeeper.

Micah had forgiven himself for being a shitty brother. But now, here, he had a chance to actually make amends. To help Kellen and keep him from losing everything in that terrible deal he'd made.

Micah left the window and crossed the library. Past

the room, he found a hallway with a bank of payphones, and beyond that, a stairwell up to the dorms. Those dorms would be his home for the next twenty-eight days. He would learn his room assignment after lunch.

He had to think for a second to remember Frank's cell number. With all his numbers stored in his phone, he didn't have any of them memorized. Micah did finally remember it, dialed, and the sandpapery sound of Frank's voice came on the other end of the line.

"Hello?"

"It's me."

"Hey, kid. How are things?"

Micah glanced around the hallway. No one on the other payphones, no one within earshot. "I'm not sure how much I should say on the phone."

Frank scoffed. "Don't worry about that. It's rehab, not jail. You introduce yourself to Snoop yet?"

"They only let me out of detox a few minutes ago. I haven't met anyone yet. It's so weird being here."

"You never went to treatment before, did you?"

"Just the detox you picked me up from. What's weird is that this mansion is so nice, like a fine hotel. But it's filled with puke-stained and rabid people, just like that detox was."

"You can put a drunk in a tuxedo, but he's still a drunk, kid."

"I look like an idiot in a tuxedo, so I have that going for me."

Frank grunted. The salty words of his boss and AA

sponsor usually had such a calming effect on Micah. But today, he had too much on his mind. "I'm not sure where I'm supposed to start with Jiménez. What do I do if this guy Snoop suspects me right away?"

"Don't worry about it. You'll be fine. Take your time, you have a couple weeks. Earn his trust. Get him to open up a little bit at a time. Once he sees he can trust you, he'll be spilling his whole life story to you. I've seen it happen with new people in recovery, plenty of times."

"Got it, boss. What are you going to be doing over the next few weeks? You temporarily shutting down Mueller Bail Enforcement?"

"I wrapped up the last outstanding bail case yesterday, so we're in the clear for now. Me and Gavin are going to chase down a lead, actually. Your boy Snoop visited an abandoned office building in Oklahoma City a couple times over the last few months. We're going to check it out."

That gave Micah some comfort, to know that Frank would be an hour away in OKC. Still, Micah's palms felt greasy, and his heart thumped in his chest. "I don't know if I can do this, Frank."

"Whaddaya mean?"

"Now that I'm here… it's not so easy. I want to do this to help my brother, but I feel like I'm among a bunch of wolves here."

"You've pretended to be someone else before."

"This feels different. There's a lot on the line."

"I get that. And maybe it's a little close to home, being

in a treatment center. But it's okay to be scared. Just don't let the fear tell you what to do. Courage isn't lack of fear. It's not letting fear dictate your actions."

Micah smiled and tugged on the payphone's cord. "I like it, Frank. I'm going to put that on a coffee mug."

"Yeah, yeah, kid."

Before Micah could respond, Oscar appeared at the end of the hallway, clipboard in hand. The nurse's eyebrows raised.

"Micah, off the phone, please. It's time for lunch."

~

Cornerstone's cafeteria was in a side building, two hundred feet from the mansion. Connected by a stone walkway that led out from the porch, the general smoking/gathering area of campus. Morning activities all let out at around 11:45, so Micah wandered through a collection of smokers and vapers as he made his way to the side building.

The inside reminded him of High School, with the clusters of rounded tables and a buffet line that snaked through the room and dipped into the kitchen. Sneeze glass covered the row of food troughs, and patients pushed plastic trays along a metal grate toward the end of the line.

After picking up his tray of chicken, corn, and mashed potatoes, he wandered out into the sea of tables, feeling even more like High School. Where to sit? With the jocks, the brainy kids, the druggies? Except here, they were all druggies. But would there be the same social cost of choosing the wrong clique on day one of social interaction? Possibly not.

He spotted Nash through the crowd, sitting next to a gangly man with a smattering of adult acne and messy hair. Since Nash was the only person Micah knew among the seventy or so residents at Cornerstone, he made a straight line for the table and slid into a chair. The gangly guy didn't lift his head.

"Hey," Micah said.

Nash gave a flick of the head, and Gangly Guy mumbled something as he picked through his corn.

"Welcome to the big leagues, Micah. Looks like we're going to be roomies again, up in the dorms."

"Oh yeah? I didn't know."

"Oscar just told me. You got a counselor yet?"

"I don't think so," Micah said. "Nobody's said anything to me."

"What I haven't been able to figure out is if they draw names out of a hat, or if they get together and talk about who's gonna take who. Likely, I'll be with old Bob again. Whoever they stick you with can make a big difference in how your twenty-eight days play out, that's for sure."

"How so?" Micah said.

"You'll be with your counselor every day at first, then every couple days after that. Bearing your soul, telling him all about how your daddy was mean to you growing up."

"Doesn't sound like fun."

Nash cackled. "Whoever said treatment was supposed to be fun?"

Gangly Guy finally lifted his head, but not to look at Micah. His eyes honed across the room, staring. Micah turned to follow the gaze and landed at a slender and lithe woman with long, blonde hair. She looked a few years younger than Micah, maybe early twenties. Her hair spilled over her shoulders as she turned and made eye contact with Micah.

Without thinking, he drew in a breath. She was beautiful. Not his usual type, but he couldn't stop looking, once he'd started. Her eyes were like blue crystal, sparkling under the fluorescent lights of the cafeteria. Seeing her, Micah had a blip of a music video moment; everyone else in the room disappeared, the lights turned soft, and Micah felt their love-song theme music fade in as the conversation of the room faded out.

"I'm gonna fuck that chick raw," Gangly Guy said.

Micah turned back around. "You think so?"

"Most definitely."

"How can you be so sure?"

"Because, dude," Gangly Guy said, "this is The Stone. Do you not know how easy it is to get laid in treatment? Girls here spread their legs like it's a sport."

Nash swallowed a hunk of chicken and pointed his fork at the girl, who was no longer paying attention to them. "That's Leighton."

"How do you know her name?" Micah said.

"She was here last time I was. A retread, just like me. She's pretty as a peach, but she got thorns like a prickle-bush. Trust me. You don't want none of that."

Micah dimmed. For a second, he'd been caught up in a moment of lust at the sight of this young woman, but, then he had to remember how dangerous it was to date someone early in recovery. He'd made that mistake before and had been burned. Fortunately, it hadn't cost him too much. That same luck might not find him again, not to mention that he'd be willfully endangering someone else's sobriety, too.

"Romances and finances," Micah said. "Two things that'll make you relapse faster than anything."

Nash and Gangly Guy eyed Micah, but only for a moment. Maybe they hadn't heard that particular twelve-step saying before.

Then, emerging from the buffet line was Santiago Jiménez, AKA Snoop. Short, skinny, dark skin and dark eyes. Exactly like the picture.

Snoop meandered through the sea of tables and for a moment, the close proximity to his target made Micah freeze. But he came to his senses and lifted a hand to get Snoop's attention. "Hey. You can sit with us."

Snoop stopped, scowling. Without a word, he had a seat and bit off half a dinner roll. He looked at each of his three table mates, sizing them up. The tattoo on Snoop's neck stretched as he swiveled around to view each of them. Head down, eyes half-lidded and weary.

"I'm Micah."

At first, Snoop said nothing. Glared across the table, instilling silence in everyone. So much of this environment reminded Micah of prison. Everyone closed off to everyone else, not wanting to make the first move to communicate.

Micah studied the tattoo on Snoop's neck, a little skull with the eyes colored blue. He knew of some Sinaloa cartel members who had the same design, only with green eyes. A regional thing.

Micah had thought that after the trial and Witness Protection, he would never have to see one of those designs or come close to one, ever again. But here he was, seeking it out. Plunging his hand into the snake hole.

"I'm Snoop," Micah's target said, and turned his attention back to his food. And that was the last word he said during the meal.

DAY 5.2

FRANK MUELLER STRETCHED in the passenger seat of Gavin's rental car, trying to get comfortable. His back ached like hell, and had ever since stepping off the plane in Oklahoma City.

"You okay?" Gavin said.

"Feel like crap. Don't ever let yourself get old."

Gavin sighed and turned off the car's dome light. "I'm not quite as young as I used to be, either. I'm catching up."

Frank let his eyes adjust to the darkness inside and now he could focus on Pine Ridge complex all around them. A cluster of three buildings with spacious parking lots in a tree-shrouded office park. Seemed abandoned and lonely.

"You know what a positive kind of person I am," Frank said. "How I'm always looking for the sunny side of things. You'd consider me a beaming example of optimism, right?"

Gavin chuckled.

"What?" Frank said.

"Frank, how long have we known each other?"

"A damn long time."

"And in all that time, I don't think I would have ever characterized you as a positive person."

"Well, crap. Now you've ruined the whole beautiful story I was going to tell. I don't know why else you brought me down here, except to talk your ear off."

Gavin laughed openly. "Fair criticism. Even so, I do appreciate you coming to OKC with me."

"Aww, hell," Frank said as he waved a dismissive hand. "It's nothing. Business is always slow before Christmas, anyway. If it can help Micah, I'm on board."

Gavin sighed at the darkened office building before them. They were stationed at the edge of the lot, far enough away to be outside the range of any surveillance cameras. For good measure, they'd parked underneath a tree with limbs that hovered over the car like a blanket.

"Tell me one thing," Frank said. "If your people already swept this office building once before, what do you expect we're going to see?"

"I know they didn't find anything, but our smallpox dealer Snoop Jiménez has been reported here at least twice in the last six months. Something about that doesn't sit right with me. You don't go into an abandoned office building for no reason."

"You have him on camera entering that building?"

Gavin shook his head. "On-campus surveillance has been disabled since the last business lease expired in this complex. Our knowledge of Snoop came second-hand from some local law enforcement agencies."

"You didn't answer my question."

"Fair enough. I expect us to find... I don't know. Some evidence that will shed some light on this smallpox business."

Frank sucked his teeth as his back pinched in pain. "Sounds like a long shot."

"I know, I know. But we've got no other promising leads. If we don't get a win here, and this smallpox ends up in the hands of someone or some group who could do a lot of damage with it... we're talking about cities being wiped out, Frank. I showed Micah the pictures because I thought he'd need a gentle nudge. I didn't think you would want to see them."

"Hell, Gavin, you don't have to sell me on the gravity aspect of it. But, could we at least park a little closer to the building? My back is killing me."

Gavin obliged by starting the car, and Frank emitted a sigh of relief.

They parked outside the front entrance, and Gavin secured his firearm. Frank hadn't thought to bring one, not that he could have taken anything with him on the plane.

"Got one of those for me?" Frank said.

"Of course, buddy. I wouldn't forget you."

Gavin handed Frank a .357 revolver, shiny and clean. "Like your cop days, right?"

Frank laughed, which ended in the wet gurgle of a cough. "Yeah, back in the stone age. When I made detective, I got to carry whatever I wanted."

"Ooh, I'm so impressed."

"You would have been if you'd seen me in my prime," Frank said, tossing a wry smile.

They exited the car and hustled up the steps to find the front double doors of the office chained. Frank tilted his head to the side, eyeing the chains. "You got bolt cutters?"

Gavin grunted, and they abandoned the front of the building. At the far side, they found a loading bay roll-up door and a regular entry door next to that. The windows looking into the building were tinted, but the lights inside were clearly off. Gavin reached into his back pocket and withdrew a small baton-like thing, then he held it up to the doorknob. He pressed it against the keyhole and thrust the device forward a few times. The door clicked. Gavin tried the handle, and it opened.

"Fancy," Frank said.

"The Marshal's service does like their toys."

Gavin and Frank entered the darkened building, guns out. Frank immediately noticed unmolested cobwebs lining the corners of the door. If someone had been here, they'd been careful enough to pay attention to leaving those small details behind.

Gavin clicked on a flashlight. In front of them, some

cubicles had been arranged in an open floor plan. The room was maybe fifty by fifty, with stairs up to the left, and side offices lining the other three edges of the room. Frank pointed at himself and then the office to the right. Gavin nodded and headed straight ahead.

As soon as they'd split up, Frank felt a splash of unease. Everything about this place suggested it was empty, but his instinct warned him that something was amiss.

The offices had floor to ceiling sliding glass doors, and Frank pulled back the door to the right office, gun raised. Across the room, Gavin opened another at the same time.

Empty.

"I'm not seeing anything," Frank said in a soft tone. "No computers, nothing in the trash cans. There's dust on the desktops. Nobody been here in a long time."

Gavin sighed. "Yeah. Let's check the upstairs. I'm not giving up so easily."

They crossed the room to trudge up the stairs and discovered a different layout to the second floor. The path diverted left and right, wrapping around a wall dead ahead. The same kind of half-height cubicles populated the visible space in either direction. Same as downstairs: lights off, no signs of any people having been here for ages.

Gavin tilted his head right, and Frank followed. That direction led them to a room full of cubicles and the entrance to what looked like a kitchen. Frank could smell something sour coming from that direction. Left-over milk or meat in the fridge, probably.

They headed back in the other direction and came to a locked door with a security pad instead of a lock. The pad had a nine-digit number entry system, with a green LED light below.

Frank knelt in front of it, traced a knuckle along the edge of the keypad. "No dust here."

"And something is pushing power to this door. The rest of the building has no electricity."

Frank held out a hand to the door and could feel a slight vibration coming from the other side. "Yeah, this is something independent. I'm guessing your fancy lock pick device can't open this sucker."

Gavin shook his head, then he ran hands around the door frame and tapped on the wall next to it. "Concrete. This is as secure as can be."

"Maybe if we had Layne here," Frank said.

"Layne?"

"Friend of Micah's, he works in corporate security. Tech whiz kind of guy. I've contracted him to help with jobs before. This is right up his alley, but he's back east, consulting for a few weeks."

"Hmm," Gavin said. "I don't know what to think about the rest of this place, but I'd be damned interested to find out what's on the other side of this door."

DAY 6

MICAH SAT ON the front step of Cornerstone, waiting for the van to pick him up for an off-campus visit to the doctor's office. All patients went into town for a full workup during their first week. To get poked and prodded and tested for STD's and other nasty things. Nash had told Micah what to expect that morning.

He cinched his jacket close against the cold breeze, nearly gagging from the stench of cigarettes that had already seeped into his clothing. Nearly everyone in The Stone gathered on the side porch to smoke between obligations. In the absence of alcohol and drugs, people here seemed to cling to nicotine with reckless abandon. And sex, too, just like Gangly Guy had said in the cafeteria. Micah hadn't experienced or seen any naughty business firsthand, but he had witnessed quite a lot of flirting and innuendos. And he'd only been among the general population for twenty-four hours.

As far as Micah could tell, the schedule went like this: breakfast, then everyone met in the basement for daily announcements. There were rows of desks opposite a raised stage with a whiteboard, just like a classroom. After announcements, people scattered off to various things, depending mostly on which week they were in.

And so far, nothing had put him in the path of Snoop. Micah had to remind himself that he had twenty-two more days to accomplish his task, but he still felt a sense of urgency to make progress with the guy. Given Snoop's frosty reception in the cafeteria the day before, it might require more effort than Micah had anticipated.

The door opened behind Micah and a woman eased on the step next to him. Micah turned his head to see Leighton, the beautiful blonde, also from the cafeteria the day before.

She slid next to him on the curb, a little too close for comfort. Her breath fogged as she exhaled. She smiled at him, and now observing her up close, Micah could see the dark circles under her eyes, the lack of color to her skin. A reminder that she was only a few days sober. Still sweating out the toxins from her body.

"I'm Leighton R."

She extended a hand, and Micah now noticed she had scribbled all over both of her hands with a Sharpie. On the back of one hand was a little drawing of a potted flower, and on the other, the word *patience*. Trailing up her forearm, the words *there is no spoon,* written in a lazy cursive.

Micah shook her hand, and she let her finger slip away from the inside of his, tracing it against his palm. A caress. He shied away, and she pivoted her body toward him, which made him pull back even further. He scooted a half an inch down the step, not enough to be obvious.

"I saw you in the cafeteria yesterday," she said. "I'm new, too."

"I think we were in adjoining recovery rooms."

She tilted her head. "Oh?"

"Yeah. Our beds must have been on opposite sides of the same wall. I could hear you talking sometimes."

"You probably heard me fighting with that big shit nurse Oscar. He can be so damn pushy sometimes. He's at a hallway-monitor level of actual power, but all he has to do is go running to the director if you piss him off."

Micah nodded, said nothing. He kinda liked Oscar but wasn't about to argue with Leighton over it.

"What's your name?" she said.

"Micah T."

"You take the MMPI yet, Micah T.?"

He shook his head. "Tomorrow morning, after breakfast."

"You're in for a fantastic time," she said as she opened a pack of cigarettes and jabbed one into her mouth. "It's like the SAT's, except all about how crazy you are instead of about trains leaving stations at different times. Three hours or so in that cafeteria, filling in little circles on a test sheet."

"I can't wait."

"Questions like: *do you sometimes want to eat dirt?*"

"Hmm," Micah said. "I do enjoy a mouthful of dirt every now and again, so I'm sure I'll do well."

She grinned. "Is this your first treatment, Micah?"

"I was in detox a little over a year ago. Grungy place in Denver."

She nodded. Lit the cigarette and let it hang from her lips as she spoke. "This will be my fourth."

"Four treatments? What's that like?"

"It sucks," she said as her cigarette trailed smoke into the air. "A couple of them, I got high the same day I walked out. That shit sneaks up on you like a ninja. One second, you're all *sobriety rah rah*, and then the next second, you're doing rails off a toilet lid in the bathroom of some shitty bar in Broken Arrow."

"An insidious disease," Micah said.

"Anyway, three of my stays have been here in Cornerstone, once at the 12 and 12 in Tulsa. This place is way better."

He almost opened his mouth to echo that he was from near Tulsa, but stopped himself. He had to be careful. Not only for the fact that he had no business messing around with an early twenty-something woman who was only a few days or weeks sober, but also because he didn't want to have to remember to whom he'd told which version of his backstory.

He had to focus. Remember that he was here for bigger reasons.

"Four treatments?" he said. "That must get expensive."

"You have no idea. Forget the college fund. If I ever squeeze out some kids, I'll start saving for their rehabs and therapy the second I come home from the hospital."

Micah recalled Nash's warning in the cafeteria from the day before, about how he should stay away from Leighton. *You don't want none of that.* The girl seemed innocent enough, though. A bit crass, but harmless.

She crossed her arms, with her elbows resting on her knees. A breeze blew stray blonde strands across her face. Micah tried not to pay attention to how adorable her little upturned nose was, or the generous curve of her breasts pressing against her close-fitting sweater. Why did she have to be so damn attractive?

Then, the door opened behind them, and Snoop came out, dragging a suitcase behind him. Before Micah could open his mouth, the van pulled up.

$\sim$

The van dropped Micah and Snoop off at one clinic and then left to take Leighton to a different doctor. She waved at him from the back seat as the van exited the parking lot. The girl had latched onto Micah, for reasons he couldn't fathom.

Seeing the van drive away without leaving a chaperone, knowing it would return to pick them up later, had been a strange sight. For a treatment center, The Stone wasn't as intense as the lockdown scenario Micah had pictured. This little town of Perkins had no airport, no bus or train station, no taxis or ride-share services, and no other real way to escape. If you were in this town without a car, you were effectively stranded.

Snoop had brought that suitcase with him as he'd stepped out of the van. Micah held the door open for him, eyeing his target.

"What's up with the suitcase?" Micah said.

Snoop averted his eyes and said nothing, only walked through the open door and set the suitcase against the wall. Micah followed him into the doctor's office, which was like a large house converted into office space. This room had definitely been someone's living room at some point in the past. Perkins was a former oil boomtown that had dried up fifty or seventy-five years before. Probably lots of abandoned houses everywhere.

A plump woman with murky red hair sitting behind a desk waved them forward, clipboard in each hand. Snoop paid her no attention, instead went to sit in one of the waiting area chairs.

She held up two clipboards. "Y'all my two check-ups from The Stone?"

Micah nodded.

"How're you feeling today?"

"Uh, I'm good," Micah said. He kept forgetting that he was pretending to be five days sober. When Micah had been literally five days sober, he'd been angry, nervous, paranoid, and sad, around the clock. Channeling that early sobriety physical and emotional state had been harder than he'd thought it would be.

"Have a seat and fill out the paperwork while you're waiting," she said.

Micah thanked her and took the clipboards, then he handed one to Snoop as he sat next to the sullen patient. Snoop's hand jittered a little as his fingers closed around the pen. Snoop breathed through his mouth, a tiny rasp with each inhale and exhale.

As Micah started to write, he noticed some text printed on the side of the pen. *Valium.* This was one of those free gifts the drug reps handed out to doctors.

Micah showed the pen to Snoop. "Ironic, right?"

Snoop glanced at it and then looked away, but Micah caught a hint of a smile, barely upturning Snoop's lips. Micah considered making a follow-up joke, but he let it go. Snoop had been nothing but stand-offish so far. A half smile was a huge leap forward.

They filled out their paperwork in silence for a full minute. Around them, nurses in colorful scrubs entered, called patients, and escorted them into the depths of the office. The receptionist's phone occasionally chirped and a clock on the wall ticked relentlessly. Otherwise, the room was quiet.

Then, Snoop spoke.

"It's baggage."

"What?"

"It's symbolic. Carrying around the baggage of my

past." He pointed at the suitcase against the wall, and Micah understood. Some kind of assignment to teach him a lesson, like how football coaches made fumble-prone players carry around a football all day long, even when not on the field.

"That seems annoying," Micah said.

"Not as annoying as holding on to all that stupid shit I can't seem to ditch."

"Good point."

"I only have to do it for this week, though."

Micah eyed his target. The sadness in his dark eyes, the way his face drooped. Micah had assumed that Snoop was another infiltrator, just as he was. A temporary tenant at The Stone whose stay was based on lies and manipulation. But the dour expression on Snoop's face seemed genuine. This guy was a wreck, in a way that seemed impossible to fake.

"You got kids?" Snoop said.

"Nope." Micah paused, then tried a lame joke. "None that I know of, anyway."

Snoop stared off into space, and Micah's remark didn't seem to register. After another silence, Snoop said, "booze or drugs?"

"Booze, mostly."

Snoop nodded. "Me too."

Another minute passed with no conversation, just the scratching of pen on paper. Micah was having fun inventing a fake medical history since no way would he record accurate information on this patient form. Gavin

Belmont had supplied Micah with a false social security number and address to use. Would be weeks before the clinic would figure it out, and he would be long gone by then.

"You ever tried to off yourself?" Snoop said.

Micah considered lying, but didn't know if he could handle the follow-through questions. "Not really. But I've done enough dangerous stuff to qualify."

"That's how I ended up here." He held out his hands as if studying the grooves in his palms. Micah glanced at Snoop's wrists, checking for scars, but didn't see anything. Then, Micah reminded himself that Snoop was former cartel. Cartel members wouldn't go out in some wussy manner like slashing their wrists.

"Did the pistol jam?" Micah said.

"No, white boy. You can't use a handgun. More likely to wound yourself and end up a vegetable."

Micah was so excited to hear Snoop talking, he pressed a little harder. "What happened?"

"I spent weeks on my plan. I couldn't reach the shotgun trigger with my hands, so I had to get creative. Set myself up in a chair. Had the shotgun, butt on the floor, barrel in my mouth. Then, hiked my feet up onto the chair and tied my shoelaces together, through the trigger guard. Knotted over the trigger. I was gonna let my feet slip off the chair, using the force to make the shoelaces pull the trigger. End of story."

Micah paused, waiting for more.

"Fucking shoelaces came untied."

The door at the other end of the room opened. "Mr. Jiménez?"

Snoop stood and cast a sour glance at Micah before moping toward the nurse in the doorway. Micah watched him walk away, now having no idea what the hell he was supposed to think about Snoop Jiménez.

DAY 7

ITTING IN HENRIETTA Dryden's office inside Cornerstone, Micah drifted off while his counselor spoke to him about the six primary feelings. On a coffee table between them were six block carvings, one for each word: *mad, sad, glad, hurt, afraid, ashamed.*

Her office window faced the woods behind the mansion. That sprawling expanse of rolling hills and pecan trees. Even in the winter, the open space still looked lush and inviting.

"Micah? Are you listening?"

He wasn't, not really. He'd been staring at her fish tank, mostly thinking of his brother, and what would happen with that crooked land deal in Las Vegas if Micah didn't succeed here. Kellen McBriar was married with two kids. Two kids that Uncle Micah had never met, and would never meet. Kellen thought Micah was dead—

killed in a car accident after testifying against the Sinaloa cartel—and it was safer for everyone that he believed it. Since Micah had dropped out of Witness Protection, he would no longer have the federal government's aid if his name or face leaked to the public. His family wouldn't be safe unless he stayed in the shadows.

"Yes, I'm listening."

Ms. Dryden was a boxy woman of about forty. Angular face with a sharp, flat nose, and pale skin. Probably a descendant of Vikings. Micah could picture her wearing a wolfskin and drinking mead out of a horn. She also sported arched eyebrows that gave her face a naturally unkind expression. Her carved, news-anchor type hair sat like a helmet on her head.

Dryden frowned at him. "I want you to check out one of the Big Books from the library and read the story in the back named *Freedom From Bondage*. It talks a lot about resentment, which I think is something you suffer from."

"When do I need to have it read by?"

"It's not a homework assignment. You can read it on your own time, and I think you'll get a lot out of it. Resentment is a poison that you drink, expecting the other person to die."

Micah had heard that saying before. And, he thought he'd maybe actually read that story once already. "I'll look into it. Most of the books to read here aren't that great, anyway."

She smiled, a shark-like bearing of teeth. "Well, we're not here to enjoy great fiction, are we?"

"Ms. Dryden, are you a recovering alcoholic?"

"I'm not. But do I need to *have* cancer to know how to treat it?"

Micah was so used to the AA program of alcoholics helping each other in a *pay-it-forward* way that he didn't like being lectured on how to stay sober by a normie. But, he had to play the part. He was only supposed to be six days sober, after all.

"I see," he said. "That makes sense. I never thought about it like that."

She eyed him and scribbled something on her notepad as she flicked a tongue across her teeth. Micah noticed she did that often. For a woman who seemed so physically well-constructed with her manicured hair and sharp business suit, she seemed to have a lot of tics.

He also wondered if she suspected him of lying. He was telling a version of the truth twice removed; he wasn't Michael McBriar, he wasn't even Micah Reed in here. He was Micah Templeton, fresh off a fake bender, enrolled at The Stone to get sober so he could return to his idyllic life as a professor at Tulsa Community College.

"Tell me about your first drink," she said.

This caught Micah off guard. He hadn't prepared a fake story for this. He started talking to break the silence, and offered her something close to the truth. "I was fourteen. My parents were out of town, and my older brother was having a party. All of his friends were over, and they were so cool. I was a kid, you know, so everything they did impressed me. They could drive, they were having sex, they were all smart and funny and were so cultured.

"My brother had given me a beer, but I hated it. I'd had sips before and couldn't get past the taste. He didn't want me to get drunk, so he hadn't let me get into anything harder. But then, one night, while my brother had disappeared somewhere with a girl, a friend of his was making these really strong margaritas. He handed me one, and by the time I was finished with it, I was seriously buzzed."

"How did that first drunk feel?"

Micah smiled, lost in the memory. "Like I had arrived. I didn't know it then, but it was what I'd been searching for my whole life. In an instant, I went from being an awkward, introverted teenager to someone who didn't give a shit what anyone else thought. I can still remember when the alcohol hit, and I turned my head, then it took the world a half second to catch up. I thought it was hilarious. And I wanted to be drunk as often as possible after that."

Micah stopped talking because the beauty of the memory faded into the recollection of the years of drunken unpleasantness that followed. Flunking out of school. Alienating his friends and family. Finding himself in the employ of the Sinaloa cartel. His best friend dying right in front of him as a result of that cartel. If he didn't stop talking now, he was going to reveal something he shouldn't say.

"How did the MMPI go?" she asked, cutting through the silence.

"Long. I've never answered so many weird questions. 'Do I think about eating dirt?' What's that all about?"

She smiled. "There's a method to it, trust me. You'll take it again before you leave, and you'll be surprised how much your graph changes."

"If you say so."

"Micah, where do you see yourself ninety days from now? Six months from now? I know it's early, but we need to start thinking about your relapse prevention program. Good intentions aren't going to keep you sober."

"Well, once I get back to Denv—I mean—Tulsa," he said, cursing himself under his breath. He tried not to look guilty, but he caught Dryden frowning at him. Damn. What a stupid, easily preventable mistake.

If she suspected him, this whole thing could crumble to the ground. And so far, things with Snoop weren't going well. Aside from that strange suicide attempt confession at the doctor's office yesterday, Snoop wouldn't speak to him. The classes and activities kept them all so busy, he barely had any time to pursue Snoop, anyway.

"What's in Denver?" she said.

"Nothing. I was just thinking about a ski trip I took there a few years ago."

She pursed her lips and scribbled more in her notebook.

~

After dinner, a bunch of the patients gathered in the lobby to pile into the assembled collection of vans. Every night, they allowed them to go off campus to the AA or NA meetings in town.

Micah, exhausted from the day's lectures and in-house meetings, wanted only to retire to his room and read the paperback he'd taken from the mansion's library. A mystery set in an old Scottish castle. In the book, five authors had been invited to play a murder mystery game, but then they all started dying off, one by one. Seemed obvious that the party host was the killer, but Micah hoped he was wrong about that.

As Micah skulked down the hallway toward the payphones and the stairs up to the dorms, Leighton came bounding toward him, a big grin on her face. She had drawn lazy circles all over her wrists and forearms today. Micah got a good look at them when she held out a note, like a coy child, all smiles and shyness.

Micah took the note, now feeling like a middle-schooler himself. The giggles emanating from this twenty-something woman weren't helping.

"What's this?" he said.

She shrugged. "Read it and find out."

He started unfolding the note, but she put her hands on top of his. "No, not now. I'm going off campus for the outside meeting. Read it soon, though, because it has to do with something happening later tonight."

"Okay, sure, Leighton, if that's what you want."

She leaned in and kissed him on the cheek, quickly, like a ninja, and then pulled back. With flushed cheeks, she giggled a little more, and then jogged up the hallway toward the mansion.

Micah watched her sleek figure disappear around the corner. He considered for a second that she might be drunk or high because she'd been eerily giddy. But, if she was high, why would she be leaving to attend an AA meeting?

Micah felt the nub of the Boba Fett action figure, hidden away in his jeans pocket. "That made a whole lot of sense, right, Boba?"

Boba Fett said nothing.

Rather than stand there in the empty hallway and try to puzzle through Leighton's motives, Micah turned and trundled his way up the stairs. All he wanted was an hour alone to think through his (total lack of) progress so far and figure out what he was supposed to do next.

Instead of peace and quiet, when Micah opened the door to his room, a startled yelp came from inside. His roommate Nash, standing in front of his dresser at the far side of the room, spun. Jabbed his hands behind his back. It happened so quickly that Micah detected only a blur of something as the hands disappeared.

"Did I scare you?" Micah said.

Nash stumbled over his words. "Naw, I just... can you give me a minute?"

Micah glanced down at Nash's waist, trying to see

what he was hiding behind his back. "You want me to wait outside?"

Nash nodded, so Micah closed the door and retreated a step, then sat against the opposite wall. What the hell was Nash the-former-rodeo-star doing in there? Jerking off? Getting caught for that would make him yelp, for sure. But he'd been standing up, near the dresser. That would be a little too freaky, if he were into that kind of thing.

A moment later, the front door opened, and Nash stepped out into the hallway, wearing a sheepish grin. "Sorry about that. You going into town?"

"Not tonight."

"Alright, partner. I gotta vamoose so I don't miss my ride. Catch you later."

Nash limped away to leave Micah there in the hall, and Micah waited until he'd descended the stairs before entering their room. Looked around. Nothing seemed weird or out of place.

"If I find any of my stuff sticky," he said to the empty room, "I am not gonna be happy."

Micah realized that while he was supposed to be getting close to Snoop to find out where the smallpox was and who he was selling it to, there was a separate angle: the buyer. It was certainly possible that the buyer was also a patient here. Maybe Snoop was waiting for the perfect chance to meet with this person.

What if Nash was the buyer, and the whole painkiller addiction thing was a smokescreen?

But, too much didn't make sense. If Snoop was in possession of the smallpox cache, why come here to treatment at all? Why the story about trying to kill himself only to fail because of untied shoelaces? Why not meet Nash or whoever at a warehouse somewhere, make the exchange, and be done with it?

Unless Snoop was waiting for someone to deliver it to *him*. That would explain why he'd come to treatment. An anonymous and hidden place for him to wait until he could receive the smallpox. But, with all the nurses and staff watching everyone, delivery to this treatment center seemed risky.

Too many unknowns.

Micah sat on his bed and dug in his pocket for the severed head of Boba Fett. Instead, he found the note Leighton had written to him. He'd already forgotten about it.

Come by my room tonight after the on-duty counselors do their sweep. Around 11 is a good time.

"I don't think so, Miss Trouble," Micah said to the room. He put the note aside and plucked Boba from his pocket. Set the little plastic bounty hunter on his knee.

"Am I thinking too hard about this Nash situation?"

Boba Fett still said nothing.

Micah put Boba back into his pocket and started exploring the room. He opened Nash's drawers and his nightstand. Checked under his bed. He even unscrewed the electrical socket fixtures and found nothing strange inside. No passports with different names. No big rolls of cash. Nothing.

So why the terror when Micah had walked into the room?

Micah considered that maybe Nash had been digging through Micah's stuff, trying to find drugs or money or something. Micah checked his dresser and his half-unpacked suitcase but didn't locate anything out of place. He couldn't find any evidence that Nash had been poking around here.

Maybe Nash was just a weird guy. Or maybe there was something Micah hadn't seen.

ONCE AGAIN, FRANK and Gavin found themselves sitting outside the Oklahoma City office building at night, staring up at darkened windows. A bag of cheddar popcorn sat between them on the center console. They took turns dipping into the bag, then stuffing handfuls into their mouths.

"I curse you and your whole family for buying this popcorn," Gavin said as he reached in to grasp more.

"I know," Frank said. "I can't stop either."

Gavin sighed as he swallowed. "I don't know if sitting here is doing any good. We've been staking out this building for, what, two hours?"

"That begs a deeper question: why are we here at all? I mean, why you and not FBI or CDC or whoever else should handle biological weapons?"

Gavin tilted his head from side to side. "It's complicated. There's no hard proof anything has been weaponized, and not really any proof of a crime for the FBI to investigate. Since Santiago Jiménez was a former fugitive that I tracked down and since Micah was my former WitSec responsibility and I'm more-or-less currently still acting as his case worker, this all falls on me. But believe me: if we find anything actionable, I'm going to call everyone down here as fast as I can."

Frank squinted at the building. So far, all they'd found was a mysteriously locked door in an otherwise abandoned building. And the room behind that door had power, while the rest of the building had been shut off. He grunted as he shifted in his seat.

"Back okay?" Gavin said.

"About as good as usual. I tell you, Gavin, I'm not going to be in the business much longer."

"Which business? Bounty hunting or bail bonds? Or flying across the country to break into office buildings?"

"Any of it. I'm ready to retire. Maybe a year, maybe less."

"You're really going to close up shop?"

"Actually, no. I'm going to cut Micah in on the business, teach him how to run it. Maybe I'll stay on as the owner until he can save some cash and buy it outright. I haven't decided yet."

Gavin swallowed a mouthful of popcorn. "If you'd told me this a year ago, I would have said you'd be throwing your money straight down the toilet. But it's pretty remarkable how he's changed. I have to admit it."

"Getting and staying sober will do that for you."

Silence blossomed for a few seconds, then Frank said, "who do you think these people are? Whoever is up there, hiding something in that building?"

"I have some theories on that. Snoop Jiménez stole this virus from the Serbians, and as far as we know, they have no idea he took it. There's been no retaliation, no claims about it being stolen or anyone taking credit for it. As far as we know, the Serbians don't want anyone to find out they ever possessed it in the first place."

"Yeah, I'd imagine they'd want to keep that quiet."

"The only people who know Snoop has it—or had it —are us and his old cartel buddies, Dos Cruces. I think he's gone off the reservation, planning to weasel them out, and the cartel knows that and wants its cut of the sale. I think they're either going to kill Snoop first, or they're going to let the sale happen and then snatch up the money or the smallpox after it goes down." Gavin pointed up at the office building. "And I think this is their base of operations."

"Makes sense," Frank said.

A light flashed across the inside of one of the darkened windows on the second floor. Just a blip of light, but the first indication the building wasn't empty.

"There we go," Gavin said as he reached under the seat and withdrew his pistol. Frank followed suit, and they were both out of the car and crossing the parking lot in a few seconds. Frank's back, knees, and ankles were all troubling him this evening. The brutal wet and cold of Oklahoma December seemed to cut right into his bones. Still, he didn't want Gavin to see him struggling so mightily, so he kept pace with his younger partner.

A heavy chain still held the front door closed, so Frank and Gavin headed for the side of the building. Frank's heart thumped in his chest, which was always a terrifying proposition in its own right. He had no idea how far he could push it before his ticker gave out on him.

As they approached the back door, Gavin flicked his pistol away from the door, which Frank took to mean Gavin intended to enter first. Frank stood behind him, gun pointed at the ground.

Gavin held his lockpick contraption against the door and had it open in five seconds, but the device was a little louder than Frank would have liked. They had no idea if they would find one person upstairs, or twenty. Might be better not to announce their arrival like a marching band, crashing cymbals and gongs.

"Be ready for anything," Gavin said.

At that moment, the vast number of unknowns weighed on Frank. They had no idea who these people upstairs were, or if they even had any connection to this smallpox weapon. All Frank knew was that Snoop had been seen here a couple times over the last few months. They might be about to rush into a mafia get-together, for all he knew.

Gavin started up the stairs, but Frank reached out

and grabbed his arm. Frank pointed his chin at the elevator next to the stairs.

"Decoy?" Gavin whispered.

Frank nodded. "Good chance they've already heard us coming, since we opened that door." He walked to the elevator and pressed the button. The doors whooshed open, Frank leaned in and pressed *2*, then they slinked up the stairs, guns out, pointed low so as not to shoot each other.

"Since the room splits up there, I'm going to take left," Frank said. "You go right, and don't get too far out of view."

Gavin gave an index-finger salute as acknowledgment. As the elevator rumbled to life and they climbed up to the second floor, Gavin rounded the bend in the staircase, with Frank on his heels. The US Marshal stepped out into darkness on the second floor, lit only by a sliver of moon slicing through the windows.

The room seemed unanimated and empty. Maybe the flashlight-wielding person had already left.

Frank waited a moment before joining Gavin in the barren space. As soon as he had, a dark figure flew from between two cubicles, tackling Gavin. Frank watched Gavin's head snap to the side as a pair of hands wrapped around his waist and dragged him to the ground. Grunts and the swishing of clothes broke the silence.

Then, the air rushed out of Frank as something smacked him in the kidney, and he also toppled to the ground. On instinct, Frank shot out a hand and grabbed hold of an ankle, then he jerked his hand and sent some figure dressed in all-black to the floor. The body thumped on the carpet, then scrambled away into the darkness.

Frank turned his head just in time to see that secret door wide open, a dim blue light emanating from inside it before a hand swung the door shut. He tried to rise to his feet just as Gavin was doing the same.

Something heavy connected with the back of Frank's head and he fell prone again. The world blacked out for a moment as a whine filled his hearing. Half a second later, he regained his senses.

A few feet away, Gavin grunted in pain, laboring to breathe. Frank watched his companion struggle to his feet and then stumble toward the stairs. Then the sound of footsteps shuffling down those stairs, and then nothing but the sound of Frank's own wheezing.

He rose to his feet and staggered over to the window, but there was nothing to see in the parking lot. No cars tearing into the street, no glint of light bouncing off faces running away. Those attackers had been there one instant, gone the next.

He watched Gavin race out in the parking lot, turn around a few times, and then seem to come to the same conclusion. His shoulders slumped as he reentered the building.

A moment later, Gavin trudged up the stairs, panting. "You okay?"

"Son of a bitch hit me in the head," Frank said as he

rubbed a hand on the base of his neck. It was already pounding, forming into a headache.

"There's definitely something going on here," Gavin said. "Something in that room."

Frank heaved a deep sigh, finally catching his breath. "You said you could get all your people down here? I think it's time to do that."

PART II

THE CASE OF THE MISSING SCISSORS

DAY 9.1

IN THE MORNING, Micah attended announcements in the Cornerstone basement. He learned he would have lectures until nine, then he would meet with Ms. Dryden afterward, then lunch, then they were to reconvene in groups to begin work on their cups.

At Cornerstone, all patients received a blank coffee mug to paint as part of their stay. Art therapy, or whatever. The idea being that you had to wait a year to come back and claim your finished cup, at the Cornerstone reunion day shindigs they held once a month.

During announcements, a girl named Chelsea sat next to him. She was short and curvy, with a waist that seemed improbably small for her body type. Also, she boasted a bright smile and eyelashes a mile long, which made her green eyes pop out of her skull like laser beams. Micah had learned her name in the cafeteria the day before when she had also sat next to him then, during lunch. She was young, no more than twenty. Pot smoker, not sure if she wanted to stay sober long-term, but was tired of getting in trouble for smoking, so she wanted to get "a handle" on things.

While Micah was listening to one of the counselors at the podium read a passage from the AA Big Book, Chelsea leaned over and drew a smiley face on his arm with a ballpoint pen. Micah grinned at it and then returned his attention to the reading. He didn't say anything.

The first lecture was done by grumpy old counselor Bob, a redneck who Micah assumed must have been sober for thirty or forty years. He lectured about code-pendency and how sick a family can get when they focus all of their attention on the alcoholic. How they sacrifice themselves to enable the alcoholic's behavior.

Micah would never get the chance to engage with his family about this topic. Sitting there, in that lecture, a profound sadness enveloped him when he realized that prospect. And that led to thoughts of his brother, which in turn, led to thoughts about the deal Micah had made with Gavin Belmont.

After that, Micah kept imagining the pictures Gavin had set in his lap, in Micah's car nine days ago. The grainy, black and white images of the effects of the N5A9 smallpox strain. The awful things it could do to a body.

Micah had to succeed at The Stone. He had no choice but to engage Snoop and recover the poison. Or, at least, figure out what the hell was going on so he could report the right information to Gavin.

After the first lecture had ended, Micah had a free hour, something he intended to use to learn about Snoop, who also had a free hour. Micah trudged up the stairs, hoping to follow the former cartel member and learn what he did with his free time. Micah had noticed Snoop's name written on the sign in/out sheet by the nurses' station lately, but he hadn't been able to get away to follow him. If Snoop was going off campus, Micah needed to know where and why.

At the top of the stairs stood Leighton, arms crossed, hip thrust to one side. Glowering at Micah. She was wearing a dress shirt, unbuttoned far enough that he could plainly see the lace of her bra. She would get a talking-to about the way she dressed, for sure. Micah had seen a woman sent to her room to change already once this week.

He smiled at Leighton as she waited for him to reach her on the stairs. The whole of the patients were making an exodus from the basement up to the ground floor.

"You look different."

She sighed as the crowd around them thinned out. "My counselor made me stop wearing makeup. I have to do it for a week."

"That's... weird."

"I know, right?" she said, "something about hiding behind a mask. It's another one of those silly things they make you do because they think you need to learn a lesson. But I don't want to talk about that."

"Okay."

"Why didn't you come to my room?" she said. "I was waiting all night for you."

Micah bit his lower lip. The note from two days ago when Leighton had asked him to stop by her room after curfew. He hadn't gone, of course, because he had no interest in messing around with a girl who was nine or ten days sober. Correction: he had an *interest*, because she was gorgeous and practically throwing herself at him, but he'd been fighting it like a trapper squaring off against a wild boar.

He shrugged. "I'm sorry. I was in bed by eleven. Long day."

"That was my birthday, you know."

"Shit. I didn't know. I'm really sorry, Leighton."

She pursed her lips and breathed through her nose. "My counselor tells me I'm supposed to share with people about how I feel. So, I want to tell you that I felt mad that you didn't come by."

Micah cleared his throat. "I hear and appreciate the words you're saying to me." That sounded like good-enough *Positive Affirmation Active Listening Therapy Speak*.

"But, it's not too late for you to get me a present."

Micah turned up his palms, unsure what to say. It's not as if he could go on the internet and order her a pair of earrings or something like that. Aside from the nearby off-campus visits and the pay phones in the hallway, external access was cut off.

"Um, did you have something specific in mind?"

She winked at him. "You should come by my room after curfew tonight and find out. My roommate got kicked out three days ago, and they still haven't given me a replacement. I have the room all to myself."

As she said that, Snoop climbed the stairs past them, and Micah watched him take a left at the top, leading outside. Micah itched to follow his target. What if Snoop was meeting with someone, deep in the woods behind Cornerstone? What if he had a hidden cell phone out there and he was going to uncover it to make contact?

"Well?" Leighton said, her grin starting to falter. She glanced down at Micah's arm, at the smiley face Chelsea had drawn there.

"I don't think that's a good idea. I'm sorry."

Her mouth fell open. "What? Are you serious?"

"I'm afraid so. It's just that… I'm trying to give sobriety a real effort this time, and relationship things have gotten me in trouble in the past."

She locked her hands on her hips, scowling. Today, she'd scrawled the word *tolerance* a few times on both of her hands. "Who said anything about a relationship? Do you think you're God's gift to women, or something like that?"

Micah was running out of excuses. And now, thirty seconds had elapsed since Snoop had escaped out that door. Their paths crossed so infrequently, Micah had to take every chance to gather intel on him.

He fumbled over his words. "If they catch us, they'll put us on a Behavioral Contract, or straight-up kick us out. Doesn't that worry you?"

She huffed and spun, then stormed up the stairs. Micah felt guilty for a moment but had to remind himself of the greater good. He raced up the stairs past her and darted left to reach the back door, but when he jumped out onto the porch, overlooking the vast woods behind Cornerstone, he couldn't see Snoop anywhere.

DAY 9.2

HENRIETTA DRYDEN FINISHED brushing her teeth in the bathroom attached to her office, the dingy little thing with grimy tile and a cracked mirror. For what the patients paid to stay here, Cornerstone never seemed to have enough money for the upkeep it needed. Maybe when they made her director, she would fix that.

The bathroom had a claw-foot tub, which was quaint and adorable, but it's not as if she would take a bath at work. It was just for show. Maybe if they cleared it out, she could install a stair climber or an elliptical machine. Something modern, like the standing desks she'd been requesting forever that never quite made it into the budget.

She rinsed her mouth out with the Listerine and studied her face in the mirror. Another day, another wrinkle. She could swear she felt ten years older after some sessions. The way these drunks and druggies constantly lied and manipulated her was like a never-ending battle. Some of them actually wanted to get well, and Dryden had to cling to them as the reason why she kept coming to work every day.

Next weekend she'd venture into Oklahoma City and get a makeover if she could get out of on-call duty. Not likely, but a girl could dream.

Her thoughts drifted to the notes from this morning's sessions that she still needed to transfer over into the new treatment plan software. Dryden didn't know what was wrong with the old software; she'd finally gotten used to it, then they decided to upgrade to the newest version, and now all the menus were different, and she didn't know where the hell anything was.

Out with the old, in with the new. Just like what happened in Guthrie.

"You said you weren't going to think about that," she whispered to her reflection in the mirror. "Guthrie is ancient history. They didn't want you, and that's that."

Satisfied that she'd explained to her reflection well enough, she left the bathroom and returned to her desk, where she had accumulated a pile of note pages from her three sessions this morning. As always, Micah Templeton had been the most interesting one. She was used to patients not trusting her. Used to them lying and keeping secrets, but there was something different about this guy. Micah had a world of activity buzzing underneath the surface.

He'd been a little frazzled today, talking about distractions, difficulty being around other patients. Trying to focus on sobriety but feeling pulled in too many directions. Pretty typical for patients in their second week. The head starts to clear, and they realize how deep in the shit of life they are. That they no longer have their drugs and alcohol to use as medicine to treat the pain.

"What's in your head, Micah?" she said to the page. "Thirty years old, never married, no kids. What aren't you telling me?"

A knock came at her door. She sighed and said, "enter."

Nurse Oscar leaned his blocky head inside her office. "Ms. Dryden?"

"Yes?"

"The director wanted me to let you know that the afternoon staff meeting has been pushed back to four."

"We have an afternoon meeting today?"

He seemed confused. "It should be on your calendar."

"Yes, of course. Thank you," she said, and then patiently waited for Oscar to pull his head back and shut the door. For some reason, Oscar seemed frightened by her. Many of them acted this way around her, and Dryden couldn't ever figure out why. She smiled. She joked at the meetings. She did all the things she'd been groomed to do to be charismatic.

Dryden checked the calendar on her computer, and there was indeed a meeting on the books at two o'clock, which would now be four. The stupid calendar program hadn't synced to her phone the way it was supposed to.

Adding the staff meeting at four would mean she would have to re-shuffle her afternoon appointments. But, that was the cost of doing business when management was incapable of pulling their heads out of their collective asses.

No matter. She didn't yet have the power to do anything about that.

A chunk of text on the page in front of her caught her attention. A brief note she'd jotted down along the edge of the page of Micah's session notes. Micah had mentioned his brother, Gavin.

The name sounded funny.

She opened her treatment plan software and searched through the session notes back to her first session with Micah, a few days ago. In the notes, he had mentioned a sister named Magdalene and a brother named *Kellen*. When asked about other family, Micah had said he had none. The brother had been around for Micah's first drunk, when his parents had been out of town.

Brother: Kellen or Gavin?

She ran a finger over her teeth, feeling the smooth surface of the enamel. This was an interesting discrepancy. Dryden's caseload was made up almost exclusively of people in their first month of sobriety. Newly sober people are often so cloudy in the head that they can't remember their own addresses or phone numbers.

But this seemed different. People don't forget the

names of their siblings. And they don't lie about it unless they have a good reason.

Dryden sat back, raised her feet onto the desk, and placed this morning's session notes on her knees. Kellen. Gavin.

"What is in your head, Micah Templeton? What are you hiding?"

Maybe it was possible that Micah had a sibling who had died many years before, a kind of dirty family secret, and saying the name had been an accident. Maybe due to his drinking, he had a sibling who refused to speak with him, and Micah had unintentionally mentioned his name during the session today.

Or maybe it was something else.

She would need to take some time to think about how to confront Micah with this, if she decided to do that. Either way, something was going on with him, and she was going to squeeze until the truth popped out.

DAY 10.1

MICAH FELT HIMSELF sinking into the chair. Giant, suede-covered thing was like a warm hug from a teddy bear. The chair was part of Cornerstone's smaller library, the one in between the main hall and the hallway that led down to the dorms. Known around as the Little Library. Some patients used this room for group meditation, or impromptu yoga sessions, or a place to sit in silent reflection with others.

The big library was in a wing of the mansion near the sunroom, but Micah hadn't ever ventured there. Little Library seemed like it had enough books to keep Micah stocked for the rest of his visit.

The mystery paperback sat in his lap, and he debated whether or not to finish it. Obviously, the host of the murder-mystery getaway was the one systematically killing off all the authors at the castle. Particularly because none of the authors seemed to suspect the host of being the murderer. Micah didn't much feel like reading, anyway, so he set it on the nightstand next to the chair for someone else to pick up.

The real reason Micah was sitting here was that it was a high traffic area, and he was hoping to catch Snoop walking past. Next to Micah's chair sat a chess table, and the plan was to ask Snoop for a game when he next came strolling through. It was the best idea Micah had invented so far. Snoop never sat anywhere close to Micah during lectures. They didn't have any group sessions together, and Snoop ate his meals with his small group clique. During between-session breaks or free periods, Snoop didn't hang out on the porch to smoke with the rest of the patients. Micah didn't even know where to find Snoop's room in the dorms. How do you make inroads with someone if you can't spend time with that person?

This would have all been so much easier if Micah could have tied Snoop to a chair and punched the location of the smallpox out of him. But, Gavin had insisted it wouldn't work that way. That subtlety and trust was the only avenue.

Micah couldn't find a way to gain access to get him talking. Micah had twenty-eight days to make an ally of Snoop, but he'd already wasted ten of them. It's not as if he could walk up to Snoop and hand him a note that read: *Hi! I'm a former drug cartel member too, so we have sooo much in common! By the way, are you in possession of a large amount of weaponized smallpox? Oh, also, where are you keeping it, and are you planning on selling it to someone while you're here? If you don't tell me where it is, my brother will lose his life savings.*

Not so much.

Chelsea with the ultra-long eyelashes wandered through the library, not even noticing Micah at first. Then, she paused and grinned at him. Thrust her hip to one side, just a little.

"Hey," she said.

"Hi, Chelsea. How are you?"

"Just got done with the MMPI. That was a beast."

"I feel your pain," he said. "And apparently, you get to take it again before you leave."

She rolled her eyes. "Seriously? I didn't even know about that."

He had no response, so they stared at each other for a second, knee-deep in awkwardness.

"So," she finally said, "I'm going to run up to my room and take a nap. You should sit with me at dinner tonight. About half my small group graduated today, so I'm going to be a little lonely."

He smiled and didn't say anything, so she curled a few fingers as a wave and left him there. Seemed like all those times Micah had desperately wanted women to pay attention to him, he'd had zero luck. But now, he was drowning in batted eyelashes and flirty notes. Such is life.

Micah had wasted most of his free period waiting for

Snoop to make an appearance, which hadn't so far happened. He hoped this wouldn't have to be another one of those lost days, because he was going to run out of those, eventually. With a sigh, he decided to give up and take a shower while he still had time before the next lecture.

He rose from the comfy chair and ambled down the hallway toward the dorms. As he neared the payphone bank, he felt an urge to call his brother, even though that would have been stupid. As far as Kellen McBriar knew, his brother Michael had died in a car crash after testifying against the Sinaloa cartel four years ago. Kellen had no idea that Micah Reed even existed.

There would be no phone calls to Kellen. Not now, not ever. Micah had to satisfy himself with the hope that if he could recover this smallpox, Gavin would keep up his end of the bargain and nullify this bad land deal that would cost Kellen everything.

Micah moseyed to the second floor of the dorms and paused outside his room. He dug into his pocket for his room key, then grinned. This wasn't a hotel. The rooms here didn't have locks on the doors.

He opened the door. Something swiped through the air.

Micah saw a hand holding a blade. A blade with an orange hilt.

The blade jabbed into Micah's side. Hot pain exploded along his midsection, and he stumbled backward until he bumped into the opposite wall. His head smacked back against the wall, momentarily making him dizzy. Blurred vision. He stared down at the handle of a pair of scissors sticking out of his gut, and a torrent of blood seeping out from the wound. White dots formed over everything he could see.

Stabbed. Someone had stabbed him.

His hand closed around the scissors, and he tried to pull them out, but the blood made his fingers slippery. He couldn't grasp it.

Was he still in danger? More attacks coming? He had to get out of here. Someone had attacked him. But if he moved, that would only make the blood rush out faster. Someone would come for him soon. Someone would help.

His eyes rolled back into his head as his body became terribly heavy. Sleep. Go to sleep, his brain told him.

Micah slid down the wall, feeling the scissor blades shift inside his body as he moved. Another burst of pain tore through him. He looped a finger inside the handle and yanked them out, then they slipped from his grip and tumbled onto the carpet.

He could feel the blood escaping his body faster now. A lightning strike of white hot agony raced all around his body. Paralyzing him.

The pain shot him to his feet, and he slid sideways along the wall until he bumped into the frame of the next door. He smacked a hand against it, trying to call for help, but his vocal cords didn't work. Only a rush of air escaped his lips. A bloody handprint. Shouldn't someone be in their room right now? Couldn't anyone come out here to save him?

Go to sleep, his mind roared. Shut down and give up.

"Help," he wheezed as he stumbled another step or two down the hallway. Without his permission, his knees buckled, and he found himself sinking to the floor.

Voices warbled behind him, but he couldn't make out the words.

Gravity pulled at him, dragging him down.

And then Micah passed out.

DAY 10.2

FRANK AND GAVIN sat, once again, staring up at the office building in Oklahoma City. The same building where they'd been attacked by assailants unknown only two nights before. Where they'd so far made no real progress aside from finding a mysteriously locked door and then getting their asses kicked.

Several places on Frank's body still hurt. Not the usual stuff, either. He lamented the fact that he'd been too old and too slow to stop the attackers in the building. Maybe he could have been more clever than to allow himself to fall into that trap in the first place, but it didn't matter now.

Frank shivered from the cold, because Gavin wouldn't run the heater when they were just sitting there. "Tomorrow's Christmas Eve."

"Yep," Gavin said.

"Your wife and kids happy about you spending the holidays halfway across the country?"

"Nope. But my family understands. They know Christmas might have to wait until mid-January. What about you?"

"I'll give my sister a call tomorrow. Nobody else in my family cares about me wishing them happy holidays."

They sat in silence for a couple minutes, and Frank couldn't help but notice that they were the only two humans in the parking lot.

"Gavin?"

"Yeah."

"Where's the cavalry?"

Gavin winced and shifted in his seat. "Here's the thing, Frank…"

Frank groaned as Gavin trailed off and didn't provide any further information. "Son of a bitch. Don't tell me you can't interest CDC, FBI, Homeland… anybody in this. Don't tell me you've gone rogue."

"No, no, it's not like that," Gavin said. "It's just that… the evidence is thin. I can't get those departments to devote the resources until I have something more concrete."

"What about the other night?"

Gavin shrugged. "We were jumped while infiltrating a building that Snoop Jiménez has been seen visiting a couple times. It's hardly a smoking gun."

"Well, that's great," Frank said, smirking. "So we're knee deep in crap, and we're on our own indefinitely.

What about the things you told Micah about his brother? Were those 'thin,' too?"

"I told Micah one hundred percent truth. I can help his brother. This is all real, Frank. Snoop either has the smallpox, or he knows where it is, or he knows where it's going to be. Just because other people in the government abandoned this investigation for lack of evidence doesn't make it any less true."

Frank felt a gnawing in the pit of his stomach. Felt a strong desire to get to Cornerstone and pull Micah out, then get the hell back to Denver so they could return to their lives.

"How strong is your feeling about all this?" Frank said.

"As strong as it can be. We're going to catch them, and this building is the key to all of it. I don't know what's going on in there, but we can't let it slip away."

"You should have told me up front that you were on your own with all this stuff."

"I know, I know. I'm sorry, Frank. I made a mistake. I thought we would have found our smoking gun by now, and then it wouldn't have mattered."

They wallowed in silence for a half hour, watching a sleeping building sit there and sleep. Frank tried not to seethe. He could almost forgive Gavin's deception. He knew what it was like to have a hunch that no one else believed. Knew what it was like to risk your reputation to pursue something everyone else had abandoned.

Those old hunches had sometimes paid off big in his cop days.

But he hated the notion of being kept in the dark. That his friend of fifteen years had felt the need to lie to him in the name of that hunch.

Frank opened his car door.

"What are you doing?" Gavin said.

"Nothing is going on up there," Frank said, pointing at the building. "If we're going to sit out here and watch the moon move across the sky, we can at least walk around a bit. My back is killing me."

Gavin raised his hands in surrender. Frank had probably inserted a little too much anger in his voice, and he wasn't even sure if he'd done so intentionally.

"Okay, Frank, let's take a walk."

They slipped out of the car and Frank cinched his jacket close. In these flatlands of central Oklahoma, the wind whipped across the plains with a bite that he kept underestimating. Cold stung at his exposed face.

He strayed down to the sidewalk and pushed on at a brisk pace, not really caring if Gavin caught up with him or not. How much had Gavin risked based on such a tiny amount of evidence?

"I'm sorry, Frank," Gavin said as he rushed to catch up with his old friend.

"From now on," Frank said, spinning around to face him. "I want to be in the loop."

"I understand."

"Micah has put a lot on the line for this."

"Speaking of, have you heard from him today?"

"Not a peep," Frank said. "Thinking we should go over to Perkins and check on him."

And as the moonlight bounced off the black windows of the empty office buildings around them, Frank thought about his protégé Micah Reed, wondered if Micah was keeping it together over there among the wolves at Cornerstone.

DAY 11

BEFORE HE OPENED his eyes, Micah heard beeping. That familiar smell of cleaning products mixed with high levels of air freshener. At first, he had no memory of anything, and all he knew was that his side ached like nothing he'd ever experienced before. A grinding pain with dulled, throbbing edges.

And he knew that the dulled edges were from pain meds. He was in a hospital.

When Micah did open his eyes, his vision filled with two uniformed police officers, standing at the edge of his bed. One white and one black, both of them long and slender, wearing crisp uniforms.

"Good morning, Mr. Templeton," the white cop said.

"Micah," he said, his voice barely above a croak.

Why were they here? Micah couldn't remember anything, but given that he was in a hospital and he could barely move, something nasty had gone down. He wasn't handcuffed to the edge of the bed, so that was a check in the *plus* column.

"I'm Officer Zell," the black cop said, "and this is Officer Gillespie."

Micah started. Gillespie. The same last name as Micah's best friend, the one who'd died in service to the Sinaloa cartel. With that memory, a flood of others came along with it. That Micah was undercover inside the treatment center in this town, that he'd been stabbed yesterday in the gut with a pair of scissors, and that he had no idea who'd pushed those scissors into his stomach. Just the shock, the blood, trying to call for help and stumbling down the hallway.

And the most unpleasant returning memory was why he was here in this little Oklahoma town in the first place. To risk his life to help his brother. And if Micah failed, his brother would lose all his money. Lose everything.

Micah blinked back into the present.

The cops had called him Micah *Templeton*, not *Reed*. That was probably a good sign, although he couldn't think straight enough to be sure. No, that was a good sign. His cover hadn't been blown yet. At least, he thought it was good.

Head so full of buzzing bees. Hard to make sense of anything.

"How are you feeling?" Gillespie said.

"Awful," Micah croaked.

Zell flipped open a small notebook and scanned

through some text, trailing a finger down the pad. "When the EMTs came to get you last night, you told them you'd been attacked with a pair of scissors. Is that true?"

Micah nodded.

"And did you see the person who'd stabbed you?"

He shook his head. As he did, he felt his body float a few inches into the air. For a moment, the sensation was glorious. Then, terrifying. Whatever they'd given him for the pain had made him as stoned as a gargoyle. Sober Micah didn't willfully take pain medication.

"Well, here's the interesting thing, Micah. We haven't recovered any scissors. You were stabbed in a residential hallway in the Cornerstone dorms. But as far as we can tell, no weapon has been recovered from the scene."

"Didn't you do a full sweep with the... what do you call it? I can't think of the word right now. Forensics?"

Gillespie cleared his throat. "We have an agreement with The Stone not to enter the physical building unless it's a life-threatening emergency."

That seemed like an odd thing. Cops usually didn't do that, did they? Micah reached a hand down to his waist to feel for his pocket so he could grab Boba Fett. He needed to ask Boba about this and get the bounty hunter's input. Except, Micah realized, he didn't have pockets. He was wearing a nightgown.

"Where's Boba?" Micah said.

Zell and Gillespie both cocked their heads and eyed him with confused frowns. "Excuse me?" Zell said.

"Nothing. Can you not go into the building because of patient anonymity?"

The two cops looked at each other before speaking. Micah felt their eyes meet, the unspoken words traveling through the ether between them.

"In a way," Gillespie said.

"But we've been working with someone there who acts as a liaison to us, and it seems that in addition to you not seeing anything, no one else saw anything. Don't you think that's strange?"

Micah knew this tactic. These cops were fishing, and not doing a great job of it, either. "I don't know. You tell me if it's strange."

Micah did have to wonder where the scissors were. If the staff at Cornerstone had done a room to room search, they should have turned up. Unless someone from outside The Stone had entered the building and done this. Security was pretty lax, with those spacious, open woods behind the mansion.

"Yes," Zell said, "it is indeed quite strange. So, do you have any information, anything at all that can shed any light on this situation?"

Above all, Micah wanted these cops not to keep poking their noses around The Stone. Didn't want Snoop to get spooked and leave before Micah could find out where the smallpox was and identify the buyer.

"I don't think I can shine a light for you," Micah said.

Zell gritted his teeth. "This is obviously a delicate situation here. We like to think we have a good relationship with Cornerstone. But a serious crime has been committed."

"And I sure hope you catch who did it. I don't know what to tell you, officers. I don't want to make a big deal of this. I just want to go back to The Stone so I can get on with my treatment. Whatever this was about, I'm sure it's over now."

Zell and Gillespie shared a look.

Micah realized he'd contradicted himself, and he couldn't remember why. Also, that he felt a strong desire to nap. His brain was a little boat floating on a sea of Vaseline, and he didn't know how much longer he could maintain the mental gymnastics required to keep these two occupied.

"Sometimes," Zell said, "we see patients do extreme things to get attention. You don't have a history of harming yourself, do you, Micah?"

An interesting angle. Wouldn't hurt to let them think he'd done it to himself. Micah shrugged and said, "like I told you already, I'm sure it's over now."

"You don't have any plans to leave town?" Zell said.

"Not for seventeen more days, until I graduate from treatment."

Zell closed his notebook and stuffed it into his shirt pocket. "I see. Well then, Micah, you focus on getting better. We'll come speak to you again, once you're a free man."

DAY 12.1

WHEN MICAH OPENED his eyes, Frank was sitting in a chair across from his hospital bed, elbow on knees and his fingers tented. His boss and AA sponsor's warm smile was like hot chocolate on a cold day.

"Hey, kid. Merry Christmas."

"Hey, boss," Micah said. He struggled to push himself up in the bed, and pain ripped his stomach apart. Didn't hurt nearly as bad as yesterday but the surprise of it made him woozy.

"Easy," Frank said. "Just because the scissors missed your major organs doesn't mean you need to do pushups to show me you're okay."

"Fair enough, no pushups. It's good to see you."

"It's a good thing you're not handcuffed to that bed. I half-expected to see guards posted outside your door when I got here."

Micah grinned, remembering his conversation with the cops yesterday. "I was thinking the same thing. I'm glad you got my message."

"I was going to come to town anyway, but when I heard your voicemail… you sounded high as a kite. I was ready to show up with my AA book, prepared to drag you off to a meeting."

Micah suddenly realized his throat was terribly dry. "How ironic would it be for me to relapse after sneaking into a treatment center?"

Frank grumbled. "Yeah, kid. That'd be a laugh riot. Anyway, you're getting out today."

"What? I can barely walk."

"Micah Templeton doesn't have insurance, and Cornerstone isn't going to pay for an extended stay unless you threaten to sue. And obviously, you're not going to sue. I called over there, pretending to be your lawyer. They were nervous as hell and got me off the phone quicker than you could spit."

"No, of course, I'm not going to sue anybody. Like I'd want my name publicly shared around. That would be a death sentence."

"Right," Frank said. "Here's the funny thing: I called back and talked to the Director of Cornerstone, and she told me that deep in your admission paperwork, there's a clause that says they're not liable for altercations with other patients." Frank dipped his head and looked Micah in the eye. "Was this Snoop?"

"I don't think so."

"But you don't know for sure. Did you see anything useful?"

"I didn't see a thing. Just the scissors coming at me, then I fell back, then I passed out. I woke up here two nights ago."

Micah had a fleeting suspicion that his roommate Nash had done this. That Nash had figured out Micah had been rummaging through his things and then decided to take Micah out. Scissors were a poor choice for a weapon, something borne out of impulsiveness. Since Micah was about to enter the room he shared with Nash when he was stabbed, his roommate doing the deed was the most logical explanation.

"Maybe it was my roommate, but I can't say that for sure. The guy is definitely sketchy, but I just don't know."

"Here's the thing," Frank said. "Gavin and I have a new theory that Snoop is acting *against* the wishes of his cartel buddies. That they haven't sanctioned any sale of the smallpox strain, and they're now trying to take it back. They may have seen you attempting to get close to him and come after you because of it."

"Dos Cruces is here in town?"

"We don't know, kid. Gavin and I are working on it, but we're not making much headway. We have what we suspect is the drop-off point for the smallpox strain, so we're going to attack it from that angle. Hopefully, it won't come to that. We still want to stop the deal before it happens. Our best shot is if you can get close to Snoop. Get him to tell you something and convince him to call it off. Stop him before he can leave town, but be careful not to push too hard, so you don't spook him. It's a tall order."

"Believe me, bossman, I'm trying. So far, he doesn't want anything to do with me. He's moody and standoff-y and hard to talk to."

One side of Frank's mouth curled up into a lopsided grin. "Sounds like a typical newly-sober drunk to me."

"That's definitely true, but not helpful."

"It's interesting to think that he's here at Cornerstone for legit reasons. He attends his treatment, offloads the smallpox, then he's on a plane out of the country, never to be seen again."

"Maybe so," Micah said. He winced and pressed the nurse call button. "I had an idea, Frank. Next week is my third week, and it's usually family week. I thought you could come stay with me."

Frank held up his hands and pointed at his wrist. "I think they might notice we're not the same skin color."

"I've been vague about my family in my paperwork and therapy sessions. I'll say I'm adopted. We can make this work, and since I'll be not-so-mobile over the next few days, I could really use the help."

Frank sat back and stared at the ceiling. Clucked his tongue a few times. "I suppose I can get Gavin to fudge the paperwork, draw up some adoption papers to put in the system."

"Works for me," Micah said. "Speaking of Gavin, do you think you could get him to bury the police investigation into this stabbing? The cops came by yesterday, and I don't even really remember what I said to them. I don't want uniformed guys hanging around Cornerstone, scaring Snoop."

"Gavin and I already made some phone calls yesterday about that. Might take some doing to put all the pieces together, but we can work on it. Did the cops who questioned you give you an idea about who they suspect?"

Micah shrugged, which sent a jolt of pain to his side. "I don't think so. It's all pretty fuzzy, but I remember bits and pieces. At one point, they suspected me of doing it to myself."

"As morbid as that sounds, it would be the best possible outcome for us. Especially because they won't be able to prove anything. No attack, no crime."

"The cops are named Zell and Gillespie. I think they're locals. They said something about Cornerstone not letting them enter the building? Sounded strange to me."

"Yeah," Frank said, "the treatment center seems to wield an enormous amount of power over this town. I imagine it's a huge part of the local economy. Either way, I'm fairly certain I can get Gavin to make some phone calls and make these two curious cops to back off."

"Thank you."

Frank took a timeout from speaking to cough up a lungful. "You ever hear of anyone getting arrested at Cornerstone for dealing?"

"No, I don't think so. I've seen people kicked out for it, but they never leave in cop cars."

"Hmm," Frank said. "Interesting."

"Do you know where the scissors are? The cops said they couldn't recover them."

Frank shrugged. "That wasn't us. We were hoping you stashed them somewhere."

"I don't know. Maybe I did, but I don't think so. I can't keep my thoughts together, Frank. I need to rest."

The old man stood and laid a warm hand on Micah's shoulder. "I'll see you soon. Hang in there, kid."

"I don't know that I have any other choice, bossman."

DAY 12.2

THE NURSES INSISTED Micah spend the next couple nights sleeping in the detox wing so they could keep a close eye on him. Micah agreed. He wasn't literally quarantined as he had been when he'd first arrived, but his mobility was limited enough that he'd spent most of that day in bed.

This time in the recovery suite, he had three roommates. Full house. They had each told him their names, but Micah was so foggy from the pain meds, he had trouble remembering them. Two young guys, one with long hair, one with short hair, and an older man who was bald. Longhair, Shorthair, and Baldy. That was all Micah could remember. Baldy was quiet, withdrawn, spent most of his time staring at the walls. He'd uttered one of the worst hard-luck stories Micah could ever remember hearing. Baldy had been trying to drink himself to death after both his wife and his daughter had committed suicide within a few months of each other. He'd only failed at his goal because he'd gotten a DUI along the way and had been court-ordered to treatment.

Longhair and Shorthair spent most of the day arguing about whether or not pot was an addictive drug. Longhair felt strongly that it was a gift from God and a spiritual experience and therefore not a drug, and Shorthair countered with an endless stream of statistics about gateway drugs and absenteeism numbers in corporate America. Micah stayed out of it. Micah had been sober long enough to know that it wasn't the *substance* that was the center of the addiction, it was the *person*.

On that first evening back, they brought him his dinner tray of chicken pot pie, and after picking at it, he lumbered into the little library to sit and watch the sunset through the window. He lifted a paperback from the nightstand next to the chair, flipped it over, and read the back. It was a sci-fi book about an alien invasion and a rag-tag group of soldiers tasked with venturing into the alien hive to detonate a nuclear bomb.

"Not really my scene," Micah said as he dropped the book back onto the nightstand. In the short amount of time he'd been here, Micah had read more pages of fiction than he had in years. But alien invasion? Not so much.

His side ached, but the pain meds had blurred it to a slow punching sensation instead of the flesh-tearing it had been previously. He kept thinking of that hand coming out of the crack in the door, bearing the scissors. Why hadn't he looked up to see the face of the person attacking him? Could the perpetrator have been someone from this Dos Cruces cartel, or maybe Nash, or maybe even Snoop? Would be strange for it to be Snoop, because they'd only ever spoken that one time, sitting in the doctor's office. Unless Snoop had been so humiliated after discussing his failed suicide attempt that he felt as if he had no choice but to take Micah out.

Back when Micah was a driver for the Sinaloa cartel, he knew plenty of thugs who would've killed someone after divulging a personal detail that could put them at a disadvantage. Maybe Snoop was that ruthless a person. Maybe Snoop was clinging to those old gangster ways of treating everyone in the world as an enemy.

People drifted through the library as Micah sat in his comfy chair and stared out the window. Some of them stopped to ask him how he was feeling, offered to pray for him, or gave him other bits of small talk. What he'd missed in Group the day before, contents of the lectures, that sort of thing. He politely declined a few offers for hugs, because he didn't want anyone to squeeze his midsection.

And then, Leighton entered the library, on her way toward the dorms. She glanced at Micah for a second and then averted her eyes. The legs of her pants swished together as she hustled across the carpet.

Micah remembered, like a slap in the face.

The hand that had been coming toward him, the hand gripping a pair of scissors, had marker scribbled on the back of it. Some flowery pattern created with a Sharpie.

DAY 12.3

"WAIT," MICAH SAID, and he strained to rise to his feet.

Leighton ignored him and increased her speed to make a hasty exit from the library, so Micah went after her. The world was foggy, and he moved through it like trying to run in waist-high swimming pool water, but he caught up to her in the hallway to the dorms.

"Damn it, Leighton, stop."

She turned, annoyed. Still wearing no makeup, still gorgeous. Her blonde hair cascaded over her shoulders in wavy streams. Her eyebrows were knitted as if in a scowl, but the corners of her lips were also pulled down. She looked ready to cry.

"We need to talk," he said, trying to catch his breath.

"About what?"

"I think you know what we need to talk about."

"Are you fucking Chelsea? Is that why you wouldn't come up to my room?"

"Wait… who? What are you talking about?"

"I saw her draw that smiley face on your arm in morning announcements. I saw the way she's been making those googly eyes at you for days now. She's pretty, isn't she? Do you like brunettes? Is that your thing?"

Micah had almost forgotten about Chelsea with the long eyelashes and the eyes like shimmering emeralds. "Are you serious? You stabbed me with a pair of scissors because of Chelsea?"

Leighton tilted her head. "I'm confused. Are you saying you're not sleeping with her?"

Micah tried to keep himself from becoming too flustered. Was bordering on a losing battle. "No, I'm not sleeping with her, but that doesn't have anything to do with anything. You could have killed me."

"It's just that my boyfriend cheated on me, and it's a serious trigger for me. My counselor and I have been working through it, but he says I have a long way to go."

"You have a boyfriend?"

"Ex-boyfriend, whatever. I don't want to argue the details with you."

Micah paused, took a breath, calmed himself. "You almost killed me, Leighton, and that's not okay."

Now she crossed her arms as she began to cry. Her lower lip trembled. "I'm sorry, Micah. I didn't mean to be so impulsive. I have a history of being inappropriate with men, and I really do want to change. I'm sorry I got so upset. I just... I just don't understand why you don't like me."

He ran a hand through his hair, trying to make sense of all this insanity. "Okay, okay, let me think a second. I do like you, Leighton. And it has nothing to do with preferring Chelsea over you. I would tell her the same thing I'm about to tell you: I can't mess around with people while I'm here, you understand? I can't do it."

"Because sobriety has to come first."

"That's right."

She paused, sniffling. "So you're not mad at me?"

No, he was actually not mad. More like thinking he needed to check the sloppy joe sauce to make sure someone hadn't dropped a few hits of acid in it. How could this person think it was okay to stab someone else in the stomach with a pair of scissors over some stupid, jealous misunderstanding?

What he actually wanted to do was rush to the payphone, call 911, and have her ass arrested. But that would mess everything up, so Micah had to eat his instinct.

"No, I'm not mad."

"We can put this behind us?"

He eyed her, considered if she would do something crazy like this again if he allowed her to get away with it this time. He had to believe she was sorry about what had happened. "Of course, we can put it behind us."

She wiped a hand under her eyes. "Friends?"

With everything he had in him, he forced a smile. "Yes, friends."

"Okay," she said, then she leaned forward and kissed him on the cheek. He would have pulled back from the kiss, but his reaction reflex was so slow, she was already withdrawing by the time he'd realized what was happening.

Now she turned and walked on toward the dorm, a little bounce in her step. As Micah ambled back toward the recovery room to collapse on his bed, he realized that whatever he did, he needed to stay the hell away from this woman.

DAY 14.1

FOUR DAYS AFTER being stabbed in the stomach with a pair of scissors, Micah felt well enough to be up and around. Nurse Oscar told him he could sleep in his own bed in the dorms tonight, and he could resume his regular treatment activities. Resume his investigation of Snoop.

Micah marveled at the fact that not a single person on the staff had brought up the scissors incident. It seemed like it had never happened. Baffling. Should have been major news, the sort of thing people talked about incessantly. Micah's bloody handprint had also been scoured from the hallway in the dorms.

And where were those scissors?

Oscar said they would wean Micah off the pain pills —which were held securely at the nurse's station, of course—and he could skip any of today's or tomorrow's activities if he didn't feel up to it.

Micah was not feeling up to it, but he had a job to do, so he struggled through the discomfort to dress for morning announcements in the basement.

And that's when he caught his first break.

Counselor Bob stood at the front of the room, giving out the counselor assignment schedules for the day. Micah could hear his booming voice from the top of the stairs. Bob was a bit of a cartoon character. He had a mustache that curled away from his face like a little girl's pigtails, and he wore cowboy shirts with turquoise buttons. He was a sweet old man who yelled almost everything he said, but he didn't have any malice in his tone.

"Steve N.!" Bob said. "See Counselor Grimes! Ten o'clock! Second floor! Room six!"

When Micah descended the stairs, quite a few people turned their heads to gawk at him. Bob ceased talking. The sudden eyes gave Micah the distinct sense of déjà vu as in one of those dreams of being caught in school in your underwear. Micah hadn't ever actually experienced one of those dreams, but he imagined this must be exactly what it felt like.

He'd done his best not to attract attention to himself so far, but being the guy who'd been stabbed by a mystery attacker could change all that. Maybe the staff would pretend nothing was out of the ordinary, but not likely that all the patients would adhere to the ruse.

"You okay?" Chelsea said from across the room, and

Micah flicked his eyes to Leighton, who wasn't paying attention. She was scribbling in her spiral notebook.

"I'm good," Micah said, lifting a hand to acknowledge the question.

"We're glad you're back, Micah," Counselor Bob said. "Please take a seat. You're interrupting the damn announcements."

Micah ducked his head and dropped into a seat, trying not to wince at the pain in his side. Sitting upright in a chair was uncomfortable, and he wanted to give up and go back upstairs to rest, but he forced himself to stay put.

And then, everyone returned their focus back to the front of the room, as if Micah was no big deal at all. Maybe he'd been wrong about becoming an infamous celebrity among the patients. He considered, for a moment, the incredible fact that Gavin seemed to have actually pulled off this coverup. The two cops from the hospital had not been back. No reporter had barged into Cornerstone to ask Micah questions. As far as Micah knew, this wasn't on the internet or in the news at all. Maybe this sort of thing happened often enough here that people hardly paid attention, and that's why the staff had barely mentioned it. Or, maybe Gavin was that good at his job. Who knew what powerful friends the Marshal had.

Micah wasn't going to draw any further attention to himself, if he could help it. Least of all, do anything that might make Snoop think Micah was someone not to be trusted or someone under scrutiny.

"There's an outside meeting tonight," Bob said, "and since everyone is healthy and able," he paused, glanced at Micah, "we're trying for one hundred percent attendance." Micah had no issue with going to the meeting tonight, since he'd already made plans to meet up with Frank at the Perkins AA club to share progress.

Micah had no progress to speak of, but he was hoping to fix that today.

At the front of the room, Bob turned a page. "Got a note about chore assignments. We have an open spot to fill."

A little chatter arose among the patients. Everyone at The Stone had a rotating "work assignment," which were therapeutic tasks; things to help fill your day. You'd be on kitchen crew or hallway sweeping crew or librarian crew or other little things. The sweeping crew was for disorganized people, kitchen crew was for people who needed to learn teamwork, and librarian crew was for… people who needed to be more bookish? Micah didn't know about that one.

"We need someone to volunteer to switch over to can-crushing duty for the rest of the week."

Micah's ears perked up. Can crushing was a two-person job, and the other person assigned to it this week was Snoop.

Micah's hand shot straight up in the air. "Counselor Bob, I'd like to volunteer."

Heads turned and frowned at him. Can crushing was the most physical of the work assignments, something they seemed to force on people with anger problems. Let them take out their frustrations on aluminum cans.

"You sure, Micah?" Bob said. "You'd have to start today and finish out the week."

Micah nodded.

"Well, okay then," Bob said.

Across the room, Snoop finally looked up from doodling in his notebook and cast narrowed eyes at Micah.

~

Can crushing took place on the east side of the cafeteria, where the driveway dipped around the building. There, a loading bay for deliveries sat hidden from the main view of the mansion. Micah circled around the building after lunch to find piles of soda cans, and next to them, two wooden beams shaped like railroad ties, with handlebars attached to the sides. About four feet tall.

The ten seconds of training he'd received from Counselor Bob went like this: *Set up them cans, then you crush 'em with the thing. Then, you throw 'em in the bin. When you're outta cans to crush, y'all can stop for the day.*

As Micah surveyed the task in front of him, a sneeze worked up from his toes. He fought it and lost, and the resulting blast sent a jolt of agony all throughout his midsection. His eyes were watering. Even in the middle of winter, those old Oklahoma allergies had resurfaced after a couple weeks back in his home state.

He hefted one of the poles, felt his stomach wound pulse from the weight. Maybe this had been a terrible idea. As he lifted it and his side howled at him, Snoop came strutting around the building.

Snoop said nothing, instead picked up his own can-crushing pole and went to work flattening cans against the concrete. He raised it, bared his teeth, and slammed down the rounded base of the pole against the can, flattening it to the ground. Some of the cans were still partially full, and soda foam shrapnel sprayed in a horizontal arc from underneath the pole.

Snoop crushed ten of these cans in the time it took Micah to flatten two.

Snoop paused, rested his hands on top of the pole, chest heaving. "I heard you got stabbed."

Micah nodded.

"That's fucked up, man. Why aren't there cops everywhere, putting this place on lockdown?"

Micah shrugged, said nothing. Besides the fact that Frank and Gavin had worked some magic to keep it quiet, Micah had come to the conclusion that Cornerstone Alcohol and Drug Treatment Center didn't have any qualms about keeping this incident low-key. A stabbing at such a prestigious wellness center? That would be bad for business. Just like how no one was ever arrested after being caught with drugs on campus. Kicked out, sure, but not arrested. Bad publicity.

"You got beef with someone?" Snoop said.

"Not really. But I know who did it."

Snoop leaned forward, the pole leaning with him. His eyes widened. "You do?"

"I'll tell you who stabbed me, but you have to keep it a secret. No one else knows."

This seemed to have piqued Snoop's interest even further. "I can keep a secret."

"It was Leighton."

"That blonde chick?"

"Yep."

"Damn, son," Snoop said. "I didn't know she had it in her. She catch you in a lie or something?"

"Something like that."

"When my ex-wife changed up her meds once, she turned all crazy on me for a couple weeks. Tried to crack a Coke bottle over my head."

Micah didn't even know Snoop had ever been married. None of Gavin's intel in their initial briefing had mentioned that.

"She thought I was sleeping with Chelsea."

"Ooh, Chelsea with the big booty? I guess if you're going to get in trouble, it might as well be over a girl like that. I'll keep my distance from both those crazy bitches from now on, though."

"Seriously, Snoop, you can't tell anybody."

Snoop thought about this for a second. "When we

were at the doctor's office that day, remember what I told you about my shoelaces?"

"I remember."

"I ain't never told anybody about that. I haven't even told Counselor Bob. I don't know why I told you. Things in my life that happened... parts of me I don't tell anybody about."

"I get it. But I can keep a secret too."

Snoop nodded appreciatively and went back to smashing cans. Micah tried to do a few, but his side felt like it was ripping open with each thrust. He checked his shirt for blood, felt under it for wetness. If Nurse Oscar discovered that Micah was out here trying to bust open his stitches, the big guy would have a fit.

"I'm used to that," Micah said, breaking the silence. "Crazy chicks, I mean. I used to run with a pretty rough crowd."

"Oh yeah, white boy? Which rough crowd was that?"

"You wouldn't believe me if I told you," Micah said, playing coy.

Snoop laughed and turned his head away, but in a moment, he seemed to have taken the bait. "Try me."

"You ever hear of the Sinaloa?"

Snoop scoffed and resumed smashing cans. "Get the fuck out of here. No way someone like you used to run with the Sinaloa cartel."

"I know what that tattoo means," Micah said, pointing to the marking on Snoop's neck.

Snoop raised an eyebrow. "Only a select group of people in the whole world know what this tattoo means."

"I'm one of those people."

"So why don't you tell me what you think you know?"

"Some of the old-school players in the Sinaloa had the same tattoo, but with green eyes. The skull means you're in it for life, and the blue represents the ocean. It means west coast. You're in Dos Cruces."

Snoop's hands gripped the pole, and for a second, Micah thought Snoop was going to cross the short divide between them and swing it like a sword. Micah knew he would have no chance of defending himself in his current state.

"I haven't claimed Dos Cruces in a long time, white boy. That's ancient history."

Micah shrugged. "It's none of my business. I'm not here to run my mouth about anyone. Like I said, I can keep a secret."

Snoop stared, and after a pause, his lips curled into a sneer. His grip tensed around the pole handles.

"I don't want any of this bullshit," Snoop said. "I'm trying to be a better person. I don't know what you know, or what you think you know, but you stay the hell away from me."

Snoop let go of the pole, which teetered and then clattered to the ground. He spun on his heels and stormed away, back toward Cornerstone.

DAY 14.2

IN THE EVENING, Micah piled into one of the vans to escape into town for an AA meeting, but he had no plans to attend it after the van dropped everyone off.

The meeting was at some kind of community center or Elks lodge or something that seemed to have part-time use as an AA clubhouse. Cinderblock walls, taped-up AA slogans everywhere. A gravel parking lot surrounded the building, with cigarette butt canisters and honest-to-God spittoons next to the front door.

Ironically, the next building over appeared to be some shit-kicking rowdy saloon. Neon beer signs in the window, the rumble of subwoofer-heavy country music pulsing through the building's walls.

A few minutes after the meeting started, Micah rose from his seat and walked out the front door. No one looked at him strangely, as this was a common practice for other Cornerstone patients. Some of them, especially the ones who were court-ordered to treatment, used these off-campus AA meetings as a chance to rendezvous with people who weren't allowed to visit them at The Stone. Some of the patients only wanted to be free of The Stone for an hour, to sit outside a different building to ingest their nicotine.

Leighton was among the smoking clique, someone who went to the outside meetings but didn't seem to take them seriously. Micah had at least been appreciative that she'd stayed away from him for the two days since he'd confronted her. He had certainly taken more care whenever opening doors lately.

Micah waved at the small cluster of meeting smokers and nearly bumped into Gangly Guy, the same person from Micah's first lunch in the cafeteria. The one who'd been so determined to have sex with Leighton. If Micah knew then what he knew now, he'd have told Gangly to watch out for stray scissors attacks.

"Hey," Gangly Guy said. Micah still didn't know his actual name.

"Evening," Micah said, looking around to locate Frank's rental car. He was supposed to be waiting for Micah in the lot.

Gangly Guy jerked his head toward a spot past the cars in the parking lot. "Can I talk to you in private for a second?"

"Um, sure."

Micah followed Gangly through the cars and away

from the rest of the smokers, near the saloon next door. Micah could hear the twang of slide guitars among the music reverberating from the building. Gangly stopped short, spun, and barked, "I know something is up with your injury."

"Is that a fact?"

"This bullshit they're selling us. I'm not buying it."

Micah bit his lower lip. "What aren't you buying?"

Gangly crossed his arms and whistled breaths in and out of his nose for a few seconds. "I can see I'm not going to get a straight answer out of you, either."

"I don't know what you're talking about."

"Word around The Stone is that you shoved those scissors into your own gut so you could take a little vacation. Get some good drugs at the hospital."

Micah shrugged. "I don't know what to tell you. I don't remember anything about that night."

"Hmm," Gangly said, puffing on his cigarette. "So, you're one of them, too."

Micah tried to think of a clever response, but Gangly didn't give him a chance. He flicked his cigarette into the gravel underfoot and strode away. Turned his head to make sure that Micah saw the snarl on his face as he darted between the cars in the lot.

"Glad we had this talk," Micah called after him, and Gangly responded with a middle finger.

Micah watched him stomp back inside, then let out a sigh of relief. That exchange could have been much worse. He was honestly surprised that Gangly had, so far, been the only person to question him about the stabbing.

That didn't matter right now, though, because Micah had things to do. He walked away from the building to search for Frank. Instead of his boss, he found Gavin Belmont sitting in a rental car. Gavin turned his head enough to nod at Micah, then he unlocked the car door.

Micah slid into the passenger seat. "Where's Frank?"

"Stomach bug. We ate at Eskimo Joe's for lunch today. Think he got food poisoning."

Micah sighed. "I miss Eskimo Joe's. I used to live about two blocks from there, in this shitty little apartment behind the plasma center. I hated it at the time, but I have sorta nostalgic feelings about it now. That's weird, right?"

"Not at all. I have fond memories of my college apartment."

"Did you eat cheese fries at Joe's?"

"No, we had burgers."

"That's a shame."

"I've buried the investigation with your girlfriend, the stabber. I had to call in a couple of favors to make this happen, so I hope it was worth it. There were two cops in particular who had to take some convincing to leave it alone."

"Zell and Gillespie?"

"That's right," Gavin said. "Fortunately for us, Cornerstone is interested in keeping this quiet as well. As far as I can tell, they've done a lot of the work for us.

But, there will be no cops coming to question you again, or her, or anyone about this."

"Thank you."

Gavin pivoted in the seat. "Still, is this woman going to be a problem? I can have some people quietly take her away. Get her transferred to a different treatment center, if you're worried she's going to insert herself and cause trouble."

Micah considered it for a moment. "No, I think I can handle her. We've come to an understanding. I'd rather not shake up anything at Cornerstone if we can help it."

Gavin's eyes darted back and forth across Micah's face. "Okay, if that's the way you want to play it."

"Besides, I've already told Snoop about it. If she suddenly disappeared, he would know something is up."

"You've talked to him? How are things going with Jiménez?"

"Not yet. First, you tell me about my brother. What are you doing to help him?"

Gavin sighed and tapped his hand on the steering wheel a few times. "Okay, Micah. I talked to a friend at the FBI. They've launched an investigation into your brother's new business partner, which has frozen his in-motion deals. Your brother is still out his money, but that could only be temporary. If the investigators find something they can charge the billionaire with, your brother can walk away."

"*If* they find something to charge him with?"

"If they don't, I have other ways I can make this bad

land deal go away. I'm working on it. It's a process, Micah. You need to be patient."

Micah nodded. Not completely satisfied with Gavin's answer, but it was a step in the right direction. "I'm not good at this."

"Good at what?"

"Getting information on the sly. It would be one thing if we could put Snoop in the back of a van and threaten him until he gave up the information."

"Believe me," Gavin said, "we tried that. If I still thought it would work, we'd be doing it. This task needs a more subtle hand."

"I know. And things are not going so well with him, to be honest. Our last conversation, he told me to stay away from him."

Gavin's mouth dropped open. "Are you serious?"

"I think I can fix this. Even though Snoop said that, he still admitted to me to being a part of Dos Cruces. And he opened up to me before about something he hasn't even told his counselor. He told me about a suicide attempt. Also that he has—or had—a wife, which is top-secret info, apparently."

"Maybe you've forgotten what's at stake here, Micah. Your subtle hand carries an enormous amount of weight and severity. Think about what this poison can do to a person. If this transaction happens and it lands in the grip of the wrong people. We're talking about thousands of casualties. A little town like Perkins? It would be wiped out in a day. Men, women, children. Dying horribly in agony."

Micah flashed back to the pictures Gavin had shown him. The bodies covered in sheets. "I know."

"You need to do better than this," Gavin said. "We're running out of time. Frank and I think Snoop didn't leave Dos Cruces on good terms, and we think they're trying to recover the smallpox strain. We now suspect he stole it *from* them, not *for* them. They may come after him. If he dies and we don't recover it—"

"I get it. That would be bad. But… there's something about this guy. I don't think he's who we think he is. He's got this gruff prison-gangster exterior, but I don't think he's a bad guy."

"He's about to make a deal for a biological weapon that could do an insane amount of societal damage. He's a bad guy, Micah."

"I know, but… there's something else going on there."

"Well, whatever. If you're not making significant progress on getting answers from him, I suggest you go out and hunt for it yourself. You're probably looking for a small container within a container. Like a gym bag with a small box inside it. Maybe the box is wrapped in duct tape or sealed with something that looks like a Ziploc baggie. If you find any object that looks suspicious, do not open it."

"Gotcha."

"I'm waiting on backup resources to assist you with a

search, but we can't stay inert until they arrive. We need action now."

"If it's at Cornerstone, it's in the woods behind the mansion. There are a hundred acres back there no one hardly ever touches."

Gavin pressed the unlock button on Micah's door. "Okay. That's a good place to start. And the next time you feel like empathizing with Snoop, just remember what's at stake here. Remember your brother. Think about what happens if he loses all his assets. What that will do to his family."

Micah gritted his teeth as pressure weighed on his chest. That feeling of being an indentured servant.

"I understand, Gavin."

"Don't forget what's important here."

Gavin kept his eyes forward as Micah opened the passenger door and left the car. Gavin still wasn't telling him everything. That much was for sure.

O N THE FIFTH day after being stabbed, Micah's wound felt much better. He didn't think he would be healthy enough to hop into the ring with his boxing partner Layne, but he'd gained enough mobility to move around without too much pain. Today he would need mobility, because he had the perfect opportunity.

Between his 9 a.m. cup painting session and lunch at noon, he had two free hours to do whatever he wanted. That was enough time to explore at least some of the vast wooded expanse behind Cornerstone, to begin to dig around for any clues that would lead Micah to the alleged smallpox stash.

As he cut through the little library, Nurse Oscar ducked into the room, having come from the hallway to the dorms. They both stopped, fifteen feet away from each other.

"Hey, Micah. How are you feeling?"

Micah glanced through the window at the clouds outside before answering. "Fine, I suppose."

"Not too much pain?"

"No, it's manageable. Feeling a lot better today, actually."

"Good, good," Oscar said as he took a packet of mints from his pocket and chewed a couple. "You know, we take the health of our patients very seriously here at The Stone. I want you to know that if there's anything you need to talk about," Oscar leaned forward a little as he said the next bit, "anything at all, that you feel like you can come to me. Right?"

Micah wasn't sure what to do with this information. Oscar seemed like a decent guy, but Micah had no desire for a heart to heart with the big nurse anytime soon. Or, maybe Oscar had this same conversation with all of the patients. Maybe he was a gossip-monger who was seeking the dirt on who was sleeping with whom.

"Sure, Oscar, I get it. I appreciate the offer."

"Anything at all," Oscar said, and now this was getting creepy.

"Understood."

Oscar slipped a phone from his pocket and gasped. "Oh, I'm late for a meeting. Excuse me, Micah."

Oscar hustled past Micah, his purple scrubs shuffling as he raced back toward the stairs up to the second floor. Micah waited in the library a moment, trying to decide if he should view the encounter as anything other than some weird, random exchange with the big guy.

Micah decided he didn't have the mental energy to ponder it anymore. For all he knew, Oscar had been hitting on him. Also, Micah was burning up his free time by standing here with his thumb up his butt.

When he stepped out onto the porch, he noticed three things right away. First, the weather had taken a sudden and sharp turn in the last day or two. He'd barely been outside during his recovery from the injury. Early December in Oklahoma could be pleasantly crisp in its coldness, but January and February were windy, clammy, and miserable. Felt like January had decided to come a couple days early. Regarding weather quality, Micah had never looked back after moving to Denver.

Second, among the thirty or so people sitting on the porch to smoke between their scheduled periods was Nash, Micah's roommate. They'd barely spoken at all in several days. Micah had stopped opening up to him since that weird incident in the room when Nash had made him wait to enter. Hiding something behind his back. Micah had intended to pursue Nash as a possible buyer in Snoop's smallpox transaction, but being stabbed had taken his priorities off-target. Micah would have to get back to that.

Nash was giving him a look, and Micah couldn't tell if it was hurt or anger on his face, or something else entirely. It only lasted for a second, as Nash quickly turned his head to speak with someone else.

And the final thing Micah noticed was Leighton, sitting on a bench, her knees brushing up against the knees of a man sitting beside her. A guy Micah recognized as having checked in a couple days ago. The long-haired, pro-pot debater among Micah's roommates during his second stay in the recovery suite.

A sweater had been draped across both of their laps, and the way their forearms disappeared underneath it, looked like they were holding hands. Public displays of affection were against the rules. They thought they were sneaky. If Oscar, or old Bob, or Dryden made an appearance out here right now, any one of them would shackle these two lovers with a Behavioral Contract without a second thought.

Leighton met Micah's eyes for a moment and then she looked away, and that was fine with Micah. He felt an enormous weight off his chest, actually. Let Leighton have someone else to consider stabbing if another girl draws a smiley face on *his* arm. Maybe the longhair would be smart and wouldn't come within ten feet of another female. Or, maybe Leighton would graduate from scissors to a steak knife, and she would aim higher next time. He shuddered.

Micah left the porch and stepped out onto the grass. Frozen blades crunched under his feet, half-caked with icy dew. He navigated past the basketball court and ventured into the woods, not sure what he was going to find, or even what exactly he was looking for.

DAY 15.2

HENRIETTA DRYDEN STOOD at her office window overlooking the back woods behind Cornerstone, flossing her teeth. The clouds above seemed ominous. She lifted a glass of water from her desk, rinsed, and swallowed.

A knock came at her door, and she stowed the floss in her pocket. Before she could respond, the door opened, and there appeared Rhonda, Cornerstone's Executive Director. She was dressed today in sheer black slacks and a bulky sweater that wasn't at all flattering. Rhonda had never been much for fashion, at least in the time Dryden had known her.

"Morning, Henrietta."

"Morning, Rhonda," Dryden said as she folded her hands over her waist. Dryden had a lot of respect for the director, almost enough that Dryden didn't want to muscle her out of her job. Almost. "What can I do for you?"

"Sorry to barge in like this, but I know you have a free period now."

"It's fine. Did you need something?"

Rhonda frowned at Dryden's computer. "It's a bit of a delicate subject, and I don't want to seem calloused."

"I'm a big girl. You can tell me."

"There've been some... comments from some of the other counselors about your notes in the treatment plan software. Your two patients who were transferred to other counselors? There wasn't anything in the notes about the last couple sessions. The counselors felt at a loss."

"I hate that stupid program," Dryden said, sighing. "I was just getting used to the old one, and we had to go and switch."

Rhonda jabbed a thumb into the air behind her. "Should I get Oscar? He's kind of a whiz when it comes to these computer things. I'm sure he'd be happy to sit down with you and go over it."

"That won't be necessary. I apologize for the over-sight, and it won't happen again."

Rhonda smiled, and Dryden smiled back, doing her best to mean it. She didn't, though, and she resented the implication that she needed another remedial computer training from Oscar, the damn nurse.

"Thank you for your time, Henrietta. I'll let you get back to it, then."

Dryden nodded and waited for Rhonda to leave, then she let all the air out of her lungs as she tried to push the conversation from her mind. She didn't want to focus on the stupid session notes. This scissors stabbing incident dominated her thoughts.

She sat at her desk and brought up Leighton R's treatment record. Scanned through her detox health reports, incident reports, treatment plan. What astounded Dryden most about the whole situation, other than the fact that Leighton hadn't been arrested, was that there was no mention of the stabbing in her paperwork. Dryden wasn't Leighton's counselor, so documenting the incident wasn't her responsibility. But there should have been *something*.

No arrest, no paper trail, no mention on the Perkins Journal and Stillwater news websites. The newspaper wouldn't have put their names in any articles because of Cornerstone's anonymity deal with them, but there should have been some mention that a person had been stabbed with a pair of scissors five days ago. Seemed like a newsworthy item.

Dryden had called the police directly yesterday, and they'd been unwilling to take her statement. Said the investigation had concluded and no charges were going to be filed. She knew the police had agreed not to enter the building without explicit permission from the director, but this had to be an extenuating circumstance. To drop it so quickly was beyond odd. And, for them to give her the cold shoulder when she'd called? Infuriating.

They'd squeezed her out of any power in the situation, just like Dryden's political career in Guthrie. And she wasn't going to let that travesty happen again. Wasn't going to feel that powerlessness at having everything she valued stolen from her. Not again.

What the hell was going on here?

Micah. He was involved, so wiping the incident off the face of the earth had been his doing.

People who came into Cornerstone under this much suspicion usually all had the same intention: to move drugs through the facility. To prey on the weak, the people trying to get sober. It made perfect sense: Micah had sold bad drugs to Leighton, or someone Leighton cared about, and she had stabbed him as retribution.

Micah was the cause. Now, Dryden had to prove it.

She searched for Micah Templeton on the internet. Millions of search results came back when she Googled his name. She added modifiers like *Oklahoma* and *Tulsa*, but there were still too many results to find anything meaningful. She checked on social media, and as far as she could tell, Micah had no Facebook or Twitter accounts.

"Who doesn't have any social media accounts?" she said to the room. She doubled down, checking other less-popular social media sites, trying variations of the name. She found some Micah Templetons, for sure, but none of them were the one staying at The Stone.

She thought back to Micah's name confusion about his brother. Gavin, or Kellen. There had still been no confrontation about that; she'd been waiting to use it as her ace when she was getting close to catching him.

She searched Gavin Templeton and Kellen Templeton, trying to find any link to a sibling named Micah. The spiderweb of results and link-holes she tumbled down made honing her search impossible.

Dryden slammed the mouse against the mousepad and sat back. Spent a few seconds picking at her teeth, running her tongue across the smooth enamel. She'd flossed only a few minutes ago, but now wasn't sure if she'd done a thorough job. She could feel a hint of gunk stuck between her molars.

"Who are you, Micah? Why can't I figure you out?"

With a sigh, she walked to the window in her office and watched Micah stroll from the porch and out into the woods behind Cornerstone. His head darted around. Looking guilty.

Patients ventured into the woods behind the mansion for two reasons: sex, or to get high. All their claims about seeking alone time or seeking space to commune with nature almost invariably turned out to be bullshit.

She had a chance to catch him in the act, which was worth more than name confusion. The chance to have something concrete on Micah T.

He was probably either waiting for his buyers or making sure no one saw him sneak away to unearth his drug stash.

Keeping her eyes on his path between the trees, she

backed up to her desk and thumbed the button to use the intercom.

"Nurses' station, this is Oscar."

"Oscar? This is Ms. Dryden."

"Hello, ma'am. What can I do for you?"

"Is Micah T. off medical restriction?"

"Yes ma'am. Micah has still got a few days of meds left here, but he's been cleared to return to activity as he sees fit."

"Understood. And is he on a free period right now?"

Dryden listened to the clacking of a keyboard for a few seconds. "Yes ma'am. He's on a free period until lunch. Hey, Ms. Dryden, I heard that you maybe wanted to get a refresher on the treatment planner soft—"

"Thank you." She thumbed the intercom button again, snatched her coat, and raced out of her office.

DAY 15.3

MICAH REACHED THE edge of the clearing behind Cornerstone and advanced into the woods. The open space behind the treatment center spread back about a hundred acres, with soft rolling hills and clusters of pecan and pine trees. Big expanses of brush underfoot like a coral reef. While patients weren't technically prohibited from exploring back here, legend had it that anyone who spent time in the woods was added to some treatment "watch list."

Brown pecan shells crunched under Micah's feet as he shuffled through the grass by the trees, and he squinted to survey his surroundings. Not sure what he was looking for. Gavin had said to hunt for something like a gym bag, but it could be a suitcase, a lockbox, a plastic container, anything. And even if Micah knew the container he was seeking, he still had to find it. Could be buried, could be nestled deep in the brush.

Micah thumbed the nub of the Boba Fett action figure hidden in his pocket. "Boba, maybe this was a terrible idea."

He focused on the ground first, checking for anywhere he might find piles of dirt indicating a dig. But there was so much ground to cover, he could spend hours wandering back here. And then, if he had to double back over it all to check the trees? He was looking at days spent searching. He only had two hours free right now, and it's not as if he could start skipping lectures to hunt around in the woods. The nurses and counselors would notice that.

Micah started to imagine the woods as a grid. If he could assign it sections, maybe he could tackle a little at a time, mark off what he'd already covered, and then eliminate areas he knew he wouldn't find anything. Frank would arrive tomorrow for family week. Together, they could cover twice as much ground.

As he stepped over a mushy downed log and came upon a clearing, at the eastern edge, he noticed a mound of dirt that didn't have any grass covering it. Seemed unnatural. He stayed within the trees lining the clearing as he traced an arc toward the mound. If the smallpox was there, no sense in letting someone see him approach it. As he neared the mound of dirt, it became obvious that it had been man-made. The tiny hill was about two feet tall, and a few twigs had been lazily placed atop it as cover. Micah searched around until he found a rock the size of his fist, and he used his makeshift spade to scrape back the dirt. He dug into the mound, sweeping it aside, making the little hill smaller with each swipe.

And then his rock hit something solid.

Micah's heart thudded in his chest. This could be it.

He reached into his back pocket and produced two latex gloves he'd pilfered from the nurse's station that morning when Oscar's head had been turned. He cleared away some of the mound, until he found a wooden box submerged in the dirt.

Would latex gloves protect him? What if the poison wasn't securely contained inside this box?

Micah balled his hands into fists to prevent them from shaking. "Okay, Micah, get ahold of yourself. This is why you're here. This is why you went to all this trouble."

He wrenched the box free of the dirt. It was an antique wooden thing, about a foot long and wide, maybe six inches deep. A small padlock was keeping it closed. Micah didn't have his lock picking tools with him, but this lock was flimsy and half rusted. He reclaimed his digging rock and smashed it against the piece of metal a couple times.

The rusted thing split in two and then tumbled into the grass.

Micah reached an unsteady and gloved hand out to lift the lid.

Inside, he found a baggie full of syringes, two spoons,

some surgical tubing, and matches. A junkie's paraphernalia kit.

"No dice," he said, and dropped the box back onto the depleted mound.

Images of Micah's brother danced in his head. What would happen to him if Micah failed here today.

He pressed on, crossing the clearing to head west. As he crested a small hill, he got a better look at the expanse of forest and realized his grid idea had been crazy. A hundred acres doesn't sound like much, but in reality, the tree-laden space around him seemed endless. Would take weeks or months of hard labor to cover it all.

But then, he noticed an oddity atop a branch of a tree, fifteen feet above the ground. Something muddy blue, definitely not a bird or an animal. Nothing natural had that shape and color.

Micah navigated through the tangled brush underfoot to reach the tree, and as he squinted, he could see the blue object was a backpack. Nestled into the crook of two intersecting branches. Could it be another drug kit?

He considered climbing. Could see a path through the branches, and it didn't look that tough. But, still a little bleary from the pain meds, he wasn't sure about his dexterity. Plus, if he had to swing, or hang, or stretch out to reach that backpack, what kind of strain would that put on his stomach wound?

He found a rock on the ground and considered hurling it, trying to knock the backpack loose. But, if the contents of the backpack weren't secured, he might crack open a container and accidentally unleash a terrible weapon on himself and whoever else was in range. He flashed back to Gavin, showing him those awful pictures of the mutilated corpses, fifteen days ago.

"What the hell am I supposed to do?"

He couldn't abandon this lead. Had to improvise. Work with the materials available. He hunted around until he found three long branches, each of them at least five feet long and thin enough to lift. Then he went back to the downed log and tore off long strips of wet, stringy bark to use as a rope. He set the branches end to end, each one overlapping the other by a few inches. Then, he used his strips to wrap the ends, joining them. When he was finished, he had a makeshift pole that was at least fifteen feet long.

"Not too shabby," he said, admiring his creation.

He grasped it by one end, hunkered down, and hoisted it into the air. His abs and stomach screamed at him. The pole lifted, bobbing from its length. The higher he raised it, the more it bobbed, and the heavier it became. He could feel his side stitches straining under the effort.

Once he'd lifted the pole high enough, he maneuvered the end point toward the backpack. He hooked one strap and jostled it. Jiggled the pole to free the backpack from its spot, nestled at the branch intersection. He pivoted the pole left to clear the backpack from the tree, when the unthinkable happened.

The farthest leg of the pole bent and snapped. *Crack*.

The backpack soared to the ground. Micah heard a crunch as it hit the hardened mess of exposed tree roots.

He gasped. Instinct told him to run away. But, if he had just unleashed smallpox on the area, would it matter if he was here or a thousand yards from here?

He dropped the pole and cautiously approached the blue backpack. Heart racing, palms sweating inside the latex gloves. He knelt beside the backpack and sniffed, but couldn't detect any foul smell. He didn't know if N5A9 would have any odor.

Micah unzipped the backpack.

Inside was a broken Jim Beam bottle, and three whiskey-soaked *Hustler* magazines.

"Seriously? Nudie mags?"

He grunted, angry, frustrated, disappointed. Then, a smile cracked his face. He realized that instead of weaponized death poison exposed to the air, a stash of porno magazines was definitely preferable.

He stood and moved away from the backpack. Headed back east, thinking he might find another of those hidden caches to explore. For ten minutes he wandered, looking up and down, but with no more foreign backpacks or mounds of suspicious dirt.

Thoughts of giving up had clouded his mind when a bird sliced across his vision. His eyes instinctively followed it, and he angled his head just enough to catch a flash of clothing. He recognized Dryden's green jacket out of the corner of his eye.

Micah kept pacing forward, trying not to let on that

he'd seen her. He pivoted around a tree and sneaked a look back to find Dryden keeping pace with him. Walkie talkie in her hand.

How long had she been back there? How much had she seen?

His path took him up a hill, the steepest one in the area. Once he crested it and found the descent on the other side even steeper, he rushed down it and then cut left quickly, hustling to put some distance between him and Dryden while he was out of view. Jogging made his wounded side ache, but he bit his lip and did his best not to yelp.

A large section of brush—like a blanket—covered an area the size of a living room, and he dropped to his knees to crawl underneath it. He watched Dryden descend the hill from his secure spot. She checked left and right, looking past him, then she kept marching down the hill. She wasn't holding the backpack or the wooden box in her hand, so she probably hadn't seen his earlier discoveries.

Micah waited until she'd reached the bottom of the hill, and then he wrenched himself free of the brush, skirted back up the hill, and returned to the mansion.

DAY 15.4

SITTING UNDER THE hoop at the basketball court, trying to catch his breath, Micah wished he could go back in time ten minutes and not have hidden from Dryden. Had been a stupid idea. At the time, he'd only thought of getting caught out in the woods without a good excuse for why he was there. Of her brandishing that backpack full of *Hustlers* and the Jim Beam bottle at him, demanding an answer as to why he'd fished it out of the tree with a MacGyvered tree-branch pole.

Now he realized how guilty it would make him look if she knew that he'd spotted her and fled. His best hope was to pretend he had been oblivious to her presence. Next time she saw him, though, there would be a conversation. No doubt.

His stomach wound ached. He stuck a hand inside his shirt to feel around at the bandage, checking for wetness.

If he'd ripped his stitches, he could expect weeks left in his recovery time, instead of days.

He pulled his hand back out and examined it. No wetness. No blood. Stitches were probably intact.

At the other end of the court, a teenager in a hoodie dribbled a basketball, shot a layup, and then scrambled to collect the ball after he'd missed the shot. He paused to study Micah, then frowned. The kid tucked the ball under his arm, shook his head, and then walked off the court, back toward the mansion.

What had that been about? Did the patients at The Stone fear Micah because of the scissors incident? Maybe they thought someone who had been stabbed was dangerous, who might complicate their attempts to get sober. *Stick with the winners* was a common coffee-mug cliché spouted by the counselors here. Micah certainly didn't act like a winner. He wasn't an outstanding patient who went out of his way to help others.

And maybe, this kid understood that Micah had been skulking through the woods, acting strangely. Back in Denver, part of Micah's AA program was to reach out to and help newly-sober drunks. He couldn't do that here. His cover meant that he was pretending to have the same short length of sobriety as they had. And that was a shame, because helping other drunks made Micah feel good. Made him feel connected to people, something he didn't often get to experience in his new life, and particularly not here at Cornerstone.

In another couple minutes, the pain in Micah's side

had dulled, and he could breathe normally. That's when Ms. Dryden appeared at the edge of the basketball court, walkie still in her hand, frowning at him.

She made a straight line to him. "Micah."

"Hi, Ms. Dryden. Turning out to be a nice day, isn't it? Maybe those clouds will burn off, and we'll get some sun."

She slipped the walkie talkie into her pocket and scowled, with hands firmly on hips. "It's time that we came to an understanding. Honesty is an important part of recovery."

"Absolutely. I agree."

Out of the corner of his vision, Micah watched Leighton appear at the far end of the basketball court. He raised an eyebrow at her. She held back at first, gripping her elbows with opposite hands like she was worried about them falling off. Nervously studying Dryden.

"Honesty," Dryden said as she dropped to one knee in front of him, "is the thing that makes the difference between long-term sobriety and a never-ending string of relapses."

"Preaching to the choir here, Ms. D."

Her face darkened, and she pointed a finger in his chest. "You haven't been upfront with me, and this tangle of lies ends, right here, right now. I want to know what you were doing in the woods before you stopped here at the basketball court."

"I was out for a walk."

"What's your brother's name?"

"Kellen."

She smiled. "Why, then, in one of your early sessions, did you tell me his name is Gavin?"

Micah froze. Had he said that? Whatever he'd done, he couldn't hesitate to reply now. "Gavin is my cousin. We were always real close, like brothers. Sorry, I must have been a little foggy that session. I don't even remember. Kellen is my brother. Gavin is my cousin, on my mom's side."

She pursed her lips. Clearly, she didn't believe him, but she didn't seem willing to push it any further.

Micah cleared his throat as weight pressed on his shoulders. How deeply had Gavin Belmont installed Micah's backstory? If Dryden went digging into his past, would she find evidence to corroborate Micah's claims?

And even if she did explore and couldn't find a cousin named Gavin, would it matter?

Breaking the silence, Leighton appeared right behind Dryden.

"Ms. Dryden?" Leighton said.

The counselor stood and took a step back, putting the three of them in a triangle. "Leighton. What are you doing here?"

"Micah went out into the open space because I asked him to. He was doing a favor for me."

Micah tilted his head and gawked at Leighton, then he checked Dryden's reaction. She didn't seem to know what to make of this sudden confession.

"I see. What was this favor?"

Leighton shifted her weight from one foot to the other and rubbed her hands together. She'd scrawled stars over both of her forearms today.

"Chris and I went back there last night, after dinner. I dropped my wallet, and I asked Micah to go look for it."

Dryden looked from Leighton to Micah and back. "Micah, is this true?"

Micah nodded. So, the longhair who had been in the recovery suite with Micah was named Chris. Micah remembered now. "Sorry, Leighton, I couldn't find your wallet."

"Well," Dryden said, chewing on her lip. She wasn't satisfied, but there wasn't much she could do about it. Instead, she gave Leighton the eye and waved her toward the mansion, and they left together.

And as she walked away, Dryden turned back to Micah and gave him one last questioning look.

DAY 16.1

MICAH WAITED IN the lobby as the fresh crop of family week guests began to pour in through the doors. Moms and dads and kids with suitcases and bags, pausing just past the entrance, gawking at the opulent marble and stone of the mansion interior. Some of them wide-eyed, some with furtive looks on their faces. Who knew what they were expecting for this family week? So many of them had been lied to and manipulated for years by the very family members they were visiting.

A young patient with a mohawk, someone Micah hadn't noticed before, crossed the room, wearing a cardboard sign hanging by a string around his neck. The sign read: *I am supposed to ask for help with things.* When the kid noticed Micah reading the sign, he sneered and stomped down the stairs into the basement.

Eventually, Frank came through that door, roller bag

in one hand and a ratty green duffel bag slung over his shoulder.

"Uncle Frank!" Micah said as he crossed the room to greet his boss and AA sponsor. He threw his arms around the old man and hugged him.

"Hey, kid," Frank whispered.

"Glad you're here," Micah whispered back. "I'm getting nowhere. We need to talk as soon as possible."

Micah pulled away and pointed Frank toward the nurses' station so Frank could check in. Frank would have to complete some forms and sit through an orientation about this week.

"Good luck with your paperwork," Micah said.

Frank chuckled. "Yeah, thanks a lot. I'll come find you after, and we can catch up."

Micah shook the old man's hand and they parted ways, for now.

Micah felt his spirits lift already. Someone who knew the real Micah; knew his real name and his real past and didn't judge him for it. A companion. Someone to talk to about all the crazy things that had happened these last sixteen days.

Micah eyed a clock on the wall and hustled toward the stairs down to the basement so he could be on time for morning announcements. But when he reached the top of the stairs, former rodeo star Nash was standing there, arms crossed, blocking Micah's path.

"Hey, Micah."

"Hey, Nash. Didn't see you in our room this morning."

"I got up early. Had some things to do." Nash flicked his head toward the nurses' station. "Who is that? The guy you was talking to."

"That's my uncle."

Nash raised an eyebrow and drew a single finger across his mustache, smoothing it. "Get out of town."

"No, it is. I was adopted by his brother. My uncle's name is Frank."

"Well, Micah, that's interesting, because I remember us having a conversation in the recovery suite about this same exact thing."

A bolt of anxiety hit Micah's spine. Conversation about what? "I'm not sure what you mean."

"Your one black friend? Remember? I asked, and you told me you got one black friend, and that was your boss, Frank."

"Yeah, well," Micah said, trying not to stammer, "he's my uncle and my boss."

Nash sucked on his teeth for a second. Micah realized this was twice in two days he'd been caught by various people in a lie. Seemed he used to be quite skilled at lying, but being sober for an extended period of time had ruined that for him. Lack of dishonesty would normally be a good thing, but not so much when he was deep undercover in a place like this.

"Excuse me, Nash, I don't want to be late for announcements."

JIM HESKETT

"Fine."

Nash stepped aside and waved a hand at the stairs, then he followed Micah down the steps and entered the basement with him. Conversations with Nash were often like this. Raised eyebrows, questioning looks, ending in silence.

Micah took a seat and surveyed the room. As the meeting began, Leighton tossed clandestine glances in his direction every few seconds. Micah was hoping for a chance to talk to Snoop today, to make some progress with his target.

Snoop, however, was not in attendance at announcements this morning. So Micah kept his head down, ignored Nash's stares and Leighton's weird looks. Tried to pretend that he was in a sealed chamber and no one could see him.

A half an hour later, Micah checked in with the nurses for his pain meds and asked for Frank's bungalow number. Family guests usually stayed in a series of brick bungalows near the dorms, since hotel space in Perkins was practically non-existent.

Micah exited from the back door of the dorms, then crossed the crunchy ground to find the bungalows. Looked like a bit of rain from yesterday evening had turned into a coating of ice overnight.

He knocked on Frank's door, and the old man ushered him in.

"How was orientation?" Micah said.

Frank hefted a suitcase onto the bed and unzipped it. "You know about the knee-to-knee?"

"The what?" Micah said as he sat on one of the two queen beds.

"Knee-to-knee. It's part of our family week classes. We each have to make a list of the things we do and don't like about each other. Then, we sit with our knees together, looking into each other's eyes, and read them while the whole group watches."

"Holy crap, that sounds terrible."

"You're telling me, kid."

Micah paused. "I'm really glad you're here, boss."

"Me too," Frank said as he finished unpacking his suitcase and sat on the opposite bed from Micah. "How's your injury holding up?"

"Getting better every day. They're weaning me off the pain meds."

"Good. Let's catch up on your investigation."

"I've been trying to get Snoop to open up to me so I can ask him about the smallpox, but I'm starting to feel like that's a losing battle. I rarely have any chances to talk to him because they keep us so busy during the days. One thing is, we do have can crushing duty together. It's the only time I can get him alone, but he didn't show up for it yesterday."

"If that angle isn't panning out, what other options do we have?"

"What's going on with you and Gavin looking into the place in Oklahoma City?"

Frank shook his head. "I don't think there's anything there. We found something strange at first, but there's been no activity since. Plus, Gavin wasn't totally up front with me about it. He made it seem like FBI and others were on their way to act as backup, but that's not the case. He's gone rogue on this one."

"I knew it," Micah said, gritting his teeth. "I got the feeling the other day he wasn't telling me everything. Had that feeling on day one, actually."

"I know you have a bad history with him, kid, but I think his heart's in the right place. Don't be angry at him."

Micah considered this for a few seconds. When Micah was in Witness Protection, Gavin had been his case worker. And Gavin had been an overbearing, micro-managing kind of handler. He was half the reason why Micah dropped out of the program to fend for his own. *Bad history* was a bit of an understatement.

"I get it, Frank. But if this is Gavin's pet project and we've got no resources, I'm not sure where we go next."

"Tell me what we don't know."

"Okay. I don't know if my counselor believes I am who I say I am. She's crazy-suspicious of me in our sessions. Also, we don't know where the smallpox strain is. We assume that Snoop either has it, or knows where it is, but we can't accept that as fact. We don't know who the buyer is. And we don't know where it came from, even. Gavin told me the other day he's not sure the Dos

Cruces cartel isn't out trying to recover it from Snoop. But one way or the other, we're running out of time."

Frank nodded and then yanked out his handkerchief to cough up a lungful. "That's all true. It's a lot of unknowns. What does your gut tell you?"

"There's a guy here named Nash. He's my roommate, and there's something wrong about him. I've been thinking he might be the buyer. Maybe we change our focus from the seller to the buyer. We wait and see where it goes, and then intercept it, since where it's coming from is such a mystery."

"I take your point, but if we wait for the deal to happen, we make our window to recover it so much smaller."

Micah shrugged. "I don't know that we have another choice."

"Okay, kid. We'll play it your way and focus our energy on the buyer. But if you see a way to make inroads with Snoop, you take it."

DAY 16.2

MICAH AND FRANK sat in the cafeteria with their trays of soup and salad. Micah had to convince Frank that the food wasn't all that bad. Frank had agreed eventually, and without grumbling too much.

Micah was especially glad to have Frank here because he'd taken to sitting alone for meals lately. Since being stabbed, the other patients had withdrawn from him. Micah usually wouldn't care, but it did seem terribly ironic; he'd been the victim of a crime, but people treated him as if he were the criminal. Maybe they assumed that if he'd been stabbed, he must have done something bad to deserve it.

"Did you go to treatment, Frank?"

"No," he said through a mouthful of food. "I got sober the old-fashioned way. Someone who cared about me and was tired of seeing me drink myself to death

160

dragged me to a meeting. Not literally kicking and screaming, but damn close enough to it. I spent a few weeks in and out, drinking but still going to meetings at the same time. You know what they say: a belly full of booze and a head full of AA don't mix. Eventually, something stuck, and I decided I wanted to take it seriously."

"Crazy that you've been sober almost as long as I've been alive."

Frank nodded, thoughtfully chewing. "The first couple years were hard. After that, you keep doing what you're doing, you keep getting what you're getting."

Micah couldn't argue with that.

Halfway through their meal, Leighton breezed through the cafeteria. Micah discreetly tugged on Frank's arm and flicked his head toward her.

"That's her?" Frank said, whispering.

Micah nodded.

"Sheesh," Frank said. "I can practically feel the crazy wafting off her from across the room. She's pretty, though, so I can see why you were blind to it at first."

"No, I knew right away. I just never assumed she had enough crazy in her to stab me with a pair of scissors."

Leighton noticed Micah, then Frank, and crossed the room, tray in hand. She paused in front of their table. Her blonde hair was corralled in a ponytail today, and Micah could see the bags under her eyes had receded. Even at a couple weeks sober, her face seemed lighter. Brighter.

"Hi," she said. She didn't make any attempt to sit with them, only stood there, her shoulders tensed.

"Hi, Leighton. This is my Uncle Frank."

She knitted her brow for a second, until Micah said, "adopted."

"Oh," she said. "Hi, Uncle Frank. Welcome to The Stone. Do you want a hug?"

"No thanks," Frank said, mouth full of lettuce.

"I heard she put you on Contract," Micah said. "I'm sorry about that."

She shrugged, rattling her lunch tray. "That's okay. I didn't want to see you get into trouble. Dryden can be such a cunt sometimes."

Frank choked a little on his food and had to cough it back up.

"Sorry, Uncle Frank," she said. "I didn't mean to offend you."

"It's okay, miss," Frank said. "I've heard a lot worse in my time."

Micah noticed Snoop, sitting alone two tables away, had now taken an interest in the conversation. He was picking through a plate of french fries, watching, but pretending he wasn't watching.

Leighton cleared her throat and flicked her head to sweep a wayward chunk of hair out of her face. "I felt bad, you know, for what I did, so I wanted to make it up to you. I don't want you to think I'm the kind of person who holds grudges. I hope this makes us square."

Leighton giving Micah an alibi was nowhere near

equal to her stabbing him in the stomach with a pair of scissors, but he wasn't going to argue the score sheet. "Sure, Leighton. We're all good."

"Chaplain Greely says that if I keep how I feel stuffed inside, it's going to keep coming out in ways I don't intend."

"That makes sense."

A pause followed. Micah expected her to walk away then, but she didn't. "What were you doing out in the woods, Micah? Why were you really out there?"

He maintained her gaze and said nothing. Frank's eyes bounced back and forth between them, silently chewing.

"You're not going to answer my question?" she said.

"No, I'm not," Micah said. He tried not to look at Snoop while he spoke. Micah kept his target in his peripheral but raised his voice to make sure Snoop could hear. "I appreciate you trying to make it right for what happened before, but I don't owe you anything. You don't owe me anything. What I was doing out there was my business, and I'm going to keep it that way."

Her lips parted, face drained of color. "Whatever," she said, and then stormed off.

"That was ballsy," Frank said under his breath. "You might wake up tonight with her standing over you, trying to shove a spoon down your throat."

"I know what I'm doing," Micah said. He glanced at Snoop, who had seen the whole thing go down. Snoop dipped a french fry in ketchup and popped it into his mouth.

And he was smiling.

⌒

To Micah's surprise, Snoop showed up for can crushing duty after lunch. Micah was six cans in, already working up a sweat and stirring up the ache in his stomach from straining his abs. But it was worth it when Snoop came around that corner and picked up his crusher pole from next to the dumpster.

"That bitch," Snoop said as he slammed a few cans, "is crazier than a pack of wild dogs locked in a closet. I can't believe what you said to her, after all that shit she did to you. You got balls as big as boulders."

"Like I'm not going to stand up for myself? Where I go is none of her business."

"What's funny to me," Snoop said, "is why there ain't been cops up in here, taking statements, hauling people in for questioning. It's like they're pretending the whole thing didn't happen."

"I told them I did it to myself, and they released me."

"Why the hell you do that?"

Micah shrugged. "I'm not a narc, and messing with the police is one of my favorite hobbies. What happened that night was between me and Leighton. I prefer to handle things internally, if you know what I mean."

Snoop paused his can crushing and stared at Micah,

his jaw switching back and forth. "I don't know what to think about you, Micah T. I mean, I know that ain't your real name. That's obvious."

A pulse of tension hit Micah's spine, and he reminded himself not to show it. Kept his eye from bulging, his eyebrows from raising, his shoulders from tensing. He took a deep breath before responding. "Obvious, is it?"

Snoop nodded. "Yep. I see how you've been clocking me, trying to get on the same work assignment as me. I ain't been here long, but I've seen the shit people run up in here. Dice games, drugs, whatever. For every person in here trying to get their head straight, there's somebody else either planning the first drink when they get out or trying to figure out their angle on the inside."

"Do I look like a hustler to you?"

"That's what I can't figure out. You said you were Sinaloa, right?"

"You've got nothing to fear from me. I'm not with them anymore."

"And I'm not with Dos Cruces anymore. If I was, I'd probably choke you out and slit your throat, because that's what they'd expect from me. That's how they trained me."

Micah gave a wan smile. "Here's to turning over a new leaf, right?"

"They'd see you as competition. But the thing is, I don't want to be like that anymore. I don't want to hurt people. I want to get my priorities right so I can handle my responsibilities and leave all this drug shit behind. I thought getting out of the cartel would make things better, but I've still been a slave to my addiction. This place has helped me see that."

"Me too."

"Counselor Bob told me that his worst day sober is still better than his best day drinking. He told me that my first week, and I thought that old bastard was crazy when I heard it. I mean, I had some fun times drinking, you know?"

Micah had heard this saying before. "Sure, I had some good times too."

"But now, I understand what he meant. When I was drinking and getting high, no matter how great things were going, I still had to feed that monkey. I still wasn't free."

"True."

"Do you want to be free, white boy?"

"I do," Micah said.

"Then tell me something: why you been following me around like a puppy, asking other people about me?"

"Maybe that's my business."

Snoop laughed and slammed the pole down onto another can. "I like you, Micah T. I don't know why, but I like you."

DAY 17

ICAH THOUGHT ALL the counselors and staff might take New Year's Eve off, but no such luck. Micah had one or two free hours a day, but besides that, Cornerstone kept him busy from morning until night. So far, family week had been even more hectic. He and Frank had to sit in group sessions about codependency and positive relationship feedback all day long.

Micah didn't know if Frank had done any undercover work back in his cop days, but he was much better at this than Micah was. After sixteen days in Cornerstone treatment, Micah still felt like an outsider. Still felt like he was on the verge of being outed as a fraud, every moment he remained within these walls.

After an action-packed morning of staring at whiteboards diagrammed with communication techniques and personality types, Micah and Frank finally had a few minutes to themselves before the next session. On their way to Dryden's office, Frank pulled Micah aside.

"There's something you should know," Frank said.

Micah leaned in close, kept his voice down. "What's up?"

"I went for a walk in the woods last night and got service on my phone. Did some research. Your counselor Ms. Dryden? There's more to her than you might think."

"How so?"

"I'm not sure if it's relevant, but it's worth mentioning. She used to be the mayor of Guthrie, but she resigned in disgrace five years ago. Big scandal. She had an affair with some staffer, husband left her and got the kids, the whole bit. It was a big shit-show."

"I had no idea she was ever anything other than a drug counselor. Do you have some way to use that to our advantage?"

"Not that I can think of. You said you thought she was suspicious of you. I'm just trying to keep you on your toes because as far as I can tell, she's ambitious as hell. I learned this lesson the hard way, back when I was a cop: a good way to get ahead is to either make a big bust or drag someone down. If she can find a reason to kick you out, that's a résumé-builder for her."

"Makes sense."

"We need to be on our guard because we're running out of time, as it is."

Micah didn't need to be reminded of that fact.

"This woman is craftier than she looks," Frank said.

"If she wants you tossed from here for whatever reason, then we're out of the loop."

"Understood," Micah said. "I think she—or someone else here on the staff—may have had something to do with why they never found the scissors Leighton used to stab me."

"Could be. One more thing. Patients here aren't allowed to have cell phones, are they?"

"Nope. It's a device-free campus."

"Then I think you're right about your roommate. When I was out in the woods, I saw Nash limping along, talking to someone. When he saw me, he ditched the phone and high-tailed it out of there."

"I don't know what's going on with him. It could make sense that he's the buyer."

"Maybe so," Frank said. "We might have no choice but to follow it from that end. Let's keep an eye on it."

With that, Micah and Frank entered Dryden's office for their family counseling session. She had a desk, but for sessions, she used a set of chairs against the opposite wall for her therapeutic space. Today, she'd added a second chair across from her. Micah and Frank sat at these chairs to form a triangle.

The counselor flipped open her notebook and showed Frank a toothy smile as they exchanged names and shook hands.

"Family week can be overwhelming," she said, "so you should know this is a safe space."

"I appreciate everything you've done for Micah,"

Frank said, without skipping a beat. "I know he can be stand-offish at times, but I can see a difference in him already. This place is working wonders for him."

Dryden eyed Micah, which gave him the impression he was supposed to respond. "Yeah, absolutely. I can tell I'm changing. Not as fast as I want, but maybe better than I'd expected."

"That's the thing," Dryden said, "about treatment. It has a habit of causing all of the truths to come bubbling up to the surface."

Frank cleared his throat as Dryden flashed that shark smile again.

DAY 18

EIGHT DAYS AFTER being stabbed with a pair of scissors, Micah barely felt any pain. He'd woken up feeling refreshed and optimistic. Never mind the fact that his roommate Nash wouldn't speak to him or even look at him as they dressed in silence. Micah didn't care. He was going to find out what was going on with Nash eventually. It was only a matter of time.

Not that he had too much time left to play with. Progress needed to happen soon.

After a morning of grueling family sessions and then lunch, Micah rounded the back of the cafeteria for assigned can crushing duty. But, on the way, he noticed something strange in the Cornerstone parking lot. Nurse Oscar crossing the grounds, weaving between cars, checking behind him. Keeping his oversized body low to the ground. Oscar didn't want to be seen.

Micah paused under the rear awning of the building, hiding in the shadows as he watched Oscar skulk toward the front entrance. Just past the pillars that marked the property's edge stood two men.

Micah squinted. When his eyes focused, he saw Zell and Gillespie, the two cops who'd questioned him after the stabbing. They were in plainclothes, standing among the hedgerow beyond the entrance's stone pillars.

Oscar took one last look behind him and passed those stone pillars. Zell and Gillespie emerged from hiding, and the three of them stood in a tight triangle. Mouths moved. Hands fluttered in the air, gesturing.

Micah had no idea what they were talking about, of course, and he'd never wanted high-tech spy equipment more than in that moment. One of those pointy microphones with the bowl around it to hone in on a faraway conversation. But, in real life, he had only a set of ears, and he was positioned too far away to hear anything.

It wouldn't have mattered if he'd had some high tech equipment, anyway, because the conversation ended as quickly as it had begun. After about a minute, Oscar turned and left. No hands were shaken. Micah couldn't tell if the meeting had gone well, or if it had been an argument. Oscar weaved back through the parking lot toward the building as Zell and Gillespie withdrew into the hedge. Micah didn't see them again, but he heard the distant grind of a car engine starting soon after.

Oscar disappeared back inside The Stone. The parking lot stilled.

Weird. What the hell had that been about?

Micah couldn't think of an easy answer, so he finished his journey to the can smashing area behind the cafeteria. With his renewed vigor, he was able to wield his crushing pole with almost no strain on his abdomen. He smashed a few cans with tentative effort and felt very little pain.

When Snoop joined him for can duty, the mysterious guy even smiled at him.

"How's family week?" Snoop said.

"Not so bad. This is your third week too, right? Where's your people?"

Snoop shrugged as he crushed a non-empty can, spewing soda foam everywhere. "Parents aren't in the picture. And when I bailed on Dos Cruces, I left all those other people behind. None of them want anything to do with me."

Micah felt a pang of sorrow for the man standing opposite him. He was such an enigma. He could be unflinchingly honest in one breath, and guarded in the next. Like a coin flip, and you never knew if you'd get heads or tails. Micah supposed he had been like that in early sobriety, too. He'd seen it in others, so maybe it wasn't actually that surprising.

The oddest thing was that Micah felt a deep desire to root for Snoop. To see him succeed. Even with this prospect of Snoop completing the sale of this terrible biological agent, Micah wanted him to get sober and have a good life. Trying to reconcile those things made

Micah's head spin.

"You going to get honest with me today?" Snoop said.

Deep in thought, this had caught Micah off guard. "What?"

"Who you are, what you want. You can tell me, white boy. You tell me why you're really here, and we can stop all this dancing around."

Snoop stared, awaiting an answer. With no idea why he was about to do this, Micah said, "I know about the smallpox."

Snoop paused his can crushing and held the pole close to his chest. "Is that right? You here to arrest me?"

Micah shook his head. "I'm not a cop. But I don't want to see anyone get hurt."

"Well, you're in luck, then. Because I don't have it. I've been telling the feds for years that I don't have it, and I never did. They hauled me in a dozen times. Threatened to deport my folks. Sweated me under bright lights, withheld food and water for hours at a time. And every one of those times, they kept acting surprised that my story didn't change. You know why it didn't change?"

Micah held his breath, waited for Snoop's inevitable response.

"Because it's the truth. I'm sorry, Micah, but I don't have what you're looking for, and I ain't the person you think I am."

As Snoop returned to smashing cans with gritted teeth, Micah stared. Had to make the decision whether this was one of those times Snoop was genuine, or guarded. Had to find the honesty in a pile of rubble.

No deception clouded Snoop's face. Only weariness.

Everything in Micah said that Snoop was telling the truth. He didn't have the smallpox.

Panic gripped Micah's chest. If the poison wasn't here, no way would Gavin believe it. Gavin wouldn't help Micah's brother, and Kellen McBriar would become broke, with three mouths to feed. Would lose his house. Would probably lose his family in the aftermath.

All because of Micah.

DAY 19

THE JANUARY DAY had been an inexplicably temperate one, so Micah and Frank dragged the chairs from inside Frank's family bungalow to the front porch so they could watch the sun disappear. Oklahoma sunsets didn't usually burn orange and purple the way they did in Colorado, but something about the wide open skies gave Micah a tinge of euphoric recall about growing up here.

Earlier that day they'd endured their knee-to-knee session. They had to look each other in the eye and reveal the painful secrets about what they liked and didn't like about the other person. And even though Micah and Frank had both fabricated the *don't like* segments, it had still been an unnerving experience. Sitting in opposite chairs so close that their knees almost touched. Looking into each other's eyes.

Frank had been Micah's AA sponsor for the whole

fifteen months he'd been sober. He'd been Micah's boss for over two years at Mueller Bail Enforcement in Denver. Micah had done the fifth step with Frank, which was AA's version of a personal inventory... he'd told Frank every dirty little secret of his past, all about his time in the cartel and the things he'd done while in their service. Horrible, regretful things. Had told Frank things Micah had thought he would take to his grave, so he could unburden his soul and prevent his secrets from having power over him.

But ten straight minutes of eye contact, sitting in a circle of twenty other people? The closeness had rattled Micah's introverted sensibilities too much. Frank had done well, though. The old man was a natural.

Micah opened his book, another paperback taken from the library. This one was about a girl hiking into Bryce Canyon National Park with her two cousins. The plot had been a little too slow and meandering, but he liked the hiking details.

"While you were meeting with your chaplain this morning," Frank said, "I spent a little time in the woods again."

Micah closed his paperback on a finger to save his place. "Oh yeah?"

"Yeah. This was probably the longest of my excursions so far. A lot of messy muck out there to deal with, a lot of dead branches and frozen leaves getting in the way."

"And I'm guessing you didn't find anything?"

Frank shook his head. "A couple cellphones not-so-discreetly stashed in the bushes. Some empty beer bottles and one glass marijuana pipe, but nothing in the neighborhood of what we're looking for."

"Figures. This is seeming more and more like a lost cause."

"Do you believe him?" Frank said.

"Snoop?"

"Yeah."

Micah chewed on his lip for a moment. "I think so. I mean, Gavin seems to be the only person convinced that Snoop Jiménez has—or ever had—this N5A9 smallpox strain. The fact that Gavin can't enlist anyone else in the government to come down here to assist him seems to contradict Gavin's theory."

"Okay," Frank said, nodding, "play it all the way through, though. If you believe Snoop is innocent, and he's only here to get sober, why didn't you pack up and leave yesterday when he told you that?"

Micah sat quietly as the sun dipped below the horizon to the west, a shimmering ball of pink among a million miles of sky.

Frank coughed. "Is it because your gut is telling you something still isn't right here at Cornerstone?"

"Yeah. I think so. But I have no idea what it is. Nash is involved somehow. I've seen a lot of people do weird, unexplainable things since I've been here."

"You think your roommate is the *seller*, not the buyer?"

"No," Micah said, "that can't be it. Would be too much of a coincidence for Snoop and Nash to both be here at the same time, if Snoop has nothing to do with the smallpox."

"I agree. So here's a scenario: Snoop is telling the truth that he doesn't have it now, but he did have it in the past, at some point. He was in Dos Cruces, stole it for them, then he had second thoughts. He sunk it to the bottom of a lake or dropped it down a mineshaft. Then he breaks with Dos Cruces and tries to disappear into obscurity."

"In that scenario, Dos Cruces would be doing everything they can to recover it. Maybe they leave him alone for a year or two and follow him, see if he changes his mind and decides to sell it."

"Good thinking, kid. An alternate theory is that he didn't steal it *for* them, he stole it *from* them. Either way, they'd be watching him. And, in those scenarios, how does the gangster cowboy Nash fit?"

Micah blew out a slow breath, considering. "He's Dos Cruces, maybe? He's here to either bring Snoop back into the fold or take him out if he doesn't play ball."

"Or maybe neither of them has anything to do with anything, and there is no smallpox cache here or anywhere. That's possible. Maybe it's just a bunch of newly-sober drunks acting as crazy as newly-sober drunks usually do. Wallowing in drama and things like that."

Out of the corner of his eye, Micah saw something

dart through the trees. Two hundred feet away. Just a blip of motion, too difficult to make out in the oncoming dusk. No sound accompanied it, and for a second, Micah dismissed the blip. Then, a creeping sense of imbalance settled over him.

"Did you see that?" Micah said.

Frank pointed over to the trees, now hazy in the dark. "Over there? I think so. Like a shadow moving too fast."

Micah stood and left the porch, with Frank shortly following him. As Micah squinted into the darkened woods, he could now definitely make out a slim figure cloaked in black, about two hundred feet closer to the mansion than Frank's bungalow.

"Think he saw us?" Micah said.

"He's not acting like it, if he did."

Micah couldn't see the face, but he could see the man's neck and hands were brown. Or were they? He squinted, not sure anymore if he could discern the skin from the clothing.

Dos Cruces cartel. Had to be.

Here to kill Snoop?

The man paused at a tree at the edge of the forest before the clearing that led to the basketball courts. From the courts, the path led in a straight shot to the back of the mansion. Micah waved Frank to the left, and then Micah skirted right so they could flank the attacker from opposite sides. Micah wasn't sure if his still-healing stomach injury would hold up to a fight, and Frank's aging fists and heart might not help much either.

One way or another, they were about to find out.

Micah crept through the grass, now within thirty feet of the man, who was leaning on the tree, observing a cluster of people sitting and smoking on the far side of the basketball court. Micah looked across at Frank, who was matching his steps.

The man pulled a long blade from a sheath on his ankle.

Frank met Micah's eyes and shook his head. Wanted Micah to back off. They weren't armed, so going up against this guy was clearly a mistake.

But, this was their first real break so far. The first chance to get some answers.

Micah looked around for something to use as a weapon, and could only see a limited collection of tree branches on the ground. He found one about two feet long and a couple inches thick. Not big or heavy enough to knock this guy out, but it might do some damage. Maybe. If he could take the stranger by surprise, Micah would have a chance.

Micah lifted the branch above his head, fifteen feet away. Kept approaching, minding that his feet didn't shuffle through the crunchy leaves on the ground. Pick up each foot, set it down slowly, pausing before pressing the full weight.

Ten feet away.

The man spun. Must have felt the air move. Raised the knife. He was wearing something sheer over his face, obscuring it. Like black pantyhose.

JIM HESKETT

The man charged at Micah, knife raised. Micah readied himself to swing his tree branch when something came flying into view from the left. A rock. It pinged against the attacker's head, which sent him stumbling through the grass toward Micah, knife out.

Frank let loose a barrage of rocks, but most of them missed.

Even being pelted with rocks, the man still charged toward Micah.

Micah quickly stepped to the side and swiped the branch down, breaking it over the intruder's head. *Crack*.

The man continued stumbling forward, barreling past Micah toward the trees. Micah snatched the nub of the branch and raced after him. He wasn't sure what he was going to do. He had no handcuffs, no zip ties, no police waiting in the wings.

The man finally lost his balance and thumped into the grass, five feet past Micah.

As Micah swung the stick, the man on the ground rolled left and hopped to his feet. He jabbed the knife forward, right at Micah's chest.

Micah leaped back. Barely managed to avoid the slash of the blade.

Frank entered Micah's field of view from the right, and the attacker now noticed the two of them. He bore down for a second, head jerking left and right. Then he pivoted, sprinting back into the trees.

Micah dropped his stick and took off after the cloaked figure. In an instant, his side pulsed with stabs of pain around the wound. His breath left him as the pain seized his whole midsection. His legs kept spinning, but he could feel his body slowing, that sensation of swimming against the current.

His head pulsed. Lungs burned. Side ached.

Micah did what he could, but wasn't able to catch up to the man who was dodging between trees. As the figure kept putting more and more distance between them, Micah gave up. Heaved a giant breath and put a hand on his side. He dipped under his shirt and felt for blood, but his fingers came back dry.

A minute later, Frank appeared at Micah's side, panting.

"You okay, kid?"

Micah gulped air so he could respond. "Yeah. I was not ready for that."

"Whatever the hell is going on here," Frank said, "this place is becoming a real nightmare."

DAY 21

MICAH WALKED FRANK out the parking lot on the last day of family week. Two days since they'd chased off the man skulking through the woods. Now Micah wished they'd followed him longer, had tried to find out where he was going. At the time, Micah's aching side had made him feel like an invalid.

They hadn't seen anything else in the woods since, and The Stone had been relatively quiet for two straight days. Micah and Frank had gone about their business, acting the part, waiting for opportunities to uncover secrets. Nothing useful had presented itself.

They paused in the parking lot, jackets cinched close on this frigid afternoon. They waited until a few other nearby patients had finished saying their goodbyes so they could talk freely.

"Can I show you something?" Micah said.

Frank turned his palms up. "Of course."

Micah led Frank off to the side of the parking lot to a fenced-in grassy area, about the size of a living room. Cornerstone's therapeutic graveyard.

Frank raised an eyebrow at the collection of home-made headstones. "What in the world is this?"

"This is where we get to practice saying goodbye."

Micah opened the little gate at the front and led Frank through the pathway to the far end, pausing in front of a rock Micah had painted blue, with red letter-ing. Frank dropped to a knee to read the words Micah had painted there.

The tombstone read:

> *Phillip "Pug" Gillespie*
> *Brother, Son, Loyal Friend*
> *You'll always be with me, but I need to keep*
>   *moving,*
> *So this is where I leave my regret*

Frank studied the words as Micah felt himself winc-ing, with tears clouding the corners of his eyes. Frank stood and put a hand on Micah's shoulder. Gave it a good squeeze. "You still miss him?"

"Not as much as I used to. For a long time, I was convinced I could have prevented what happened to him if I'd done things differently. I know we talked about it when I did my fifth step, but it's still there sometimes. The regret."

"It wasn't your fault. The Sinaloa cartel did this, not you."

Micah wiped a trickle of snot from his nose. "I know. Just like I learned that forgiving someone doesn't mean excusing bad behavior, I know that refusing to forgive myself means I think I'm not worthy of forgiveness."

"And it's progress, not perfection, kid."

"I know that one too," Micah said, smiling and wiping the corners of his eyes. "Anyway, I just wanted to show you that. I made it last week, during the grief lecture."

"Well, looks like sending you here wasn't a total waste of the government's money, no matter what happens."

"Hmm. Well, I do enjoy wasting the government's money, but after Counselor Bob shouts something at you ten or fifteen times, it starts to sink in."

A chill bit the air, and Micah dug his hands in his pockets. He flicked his head back toward the parking lot and led Frank out of the little graveyard. They strolled toward Frank's car, Micah feeling that same awkward and ecstatic emptiness he felt after confessing his secrets during his fifth step.

They stopped at Frank's car and stared at each other as the nearby conversations of other patients saying goodbye faded into the background.

"I'm stalled," Micah said. "I'm down to my last week."

"Keep your head down and your eyes open. I'll be at the Motel 6 up the road in Stillwater, and I'm going to keep working on tracing Snoop's connections. There has to be something we're missing. Something simple." Frank leveled a finger at Micah. "And most of all, watch out for your counselor Dryden. She's as quick as a whip, and she knows you're not who you say you are. If you manage to get kicked out of here, not only does it cut you off from Snoop, it makes him think someone else is onto him. He's starting to trust you, and if you disappear, he'll bolt too. I guarantee it."

"I feel like we haven't gotten any closer, this whole time."

"Not true," Frank said. "We know something is very wrong here. And it's entirely possible that this smallpox transaction is still going down. If you believe Snoop doesn't have it, maybe there's something else he knows. There has to be a good reason he's leaving the country seven days from now."

"Maybe he really does want to start over."

Frank shrugged. "Maybe so, kid. But trust no one and keep at it."

"I can't stop thinking about my brother. Worrying about him and what's going to happen to him. Worrying that I might have screwed things up for him. I can't handle the fact that him losing everything could be my fault."

"Accept the things you can't change, kid, and find the courage to change the things you can. But sometimes, the hardest part is having the wisdom to know the difference. I'll be at the other end of a phone, whenever you need me."

Frank turned but then stopped short. "One more

thing: are you sure it's a good idea to leave Pug's real name on that tombstone back there? I mean, it's not likely, but suppose someone from the Sinaloa comes through here? They recognize his name, find out when it was made, find your name on a chart somewhere, then they figure out you didn't actually die in a car crash after the trial."

"You're right, Frank. I'll paint over his name. I wanted to do one honest thing while I was here, at least."

"I understand. Believe me, I understand."

Micah smiled a sad smile and opened Frank's car door for him. "And it doesn't matter, it's just a rock sitting in a garden."

"No, the rock doesn't matter at all. But the gesture means everything."

"Thanks, boss."

"Keep your head up, kid."

Micah gave his boss a hug and helped him into the rental car, then stepped back as the tires churned gravel on their way out of the parking lot.

Once again, Micah was alone.

∾

As US Marshal Gavin Belmont patrolled the exterior of the abandoned office building in Oklahoma City, he struggled not to feel guilty. The checklist in his head kept growing longer. He couldn't persuade anyone back in Washington to send him resources to continue this investigation. Gavin's boss was annoyed that he was shirking his regular duties to pursue it. He'd missed both Christmas and New Years with his wife and kids, and had to wish them happy holidays over video chat. He'd put Frank Mueller, one of Gavin's oldest friends, directly in harm's way by coaxing him to enter this building on a failed raid.

And then, there was Micah. Gavin and Micah had endured the most adversarial of relationships for the first couple years they'd known each other. Micah often accused Gavin of "micromanaging" him as his WitSec case worker in Denver. That accusation hurt Gavin deeply because he wanted only to see the young man succeed. Had he taken Micah's defiance and sullen outbursts personally? Probably. Maybe he'd retaliated against the kid by watching him too closely. After arriving in Denver and commencing to work for Frank, Micah had descended into a relentless series of relapses and alcohol binges, each one worse than the last.

Gavin had given up and allowed Micah to drop out of WitSec when he'd asked. Gavin had assumed Micah would either drink himself to death or do something stupid and get himself caught by his old crew.

Gavin paused outside the back door of the office building, gazing inside at the barren remains of a place where people used to work.

Could he have helped Micah's brother out of his bad real estate deal without involving Micah? Absolutely. Would Micah have offered to help Gavin in return, out of the goodness of his heart? The old Micah wouldn't have, that much was for sure. But this new Micah, this one who'd been sober more than a year? He genuinely seemed to have changed. Wasn't the same sullen, argumentative, manipulative person Gavin had smuggled to a new life in Denver after testifying against the Sinaloa cartel.

Now, he'd put Micah in this position to investigate Snoop Jiménez and the smallpox strain with hardly any evidence. Put his life at risk.

Maybe Gavin was the one acting selfishly now.

Gavin drew his service weapon and lock-picked the back door of the office building, then he aimed his weapon low as he crept up the stairs. There had been no sounds, no hint of movement anywhere. Last time Gavin had come through here, he and Frank had been blind-sided at the top of these stairs.

Attacked by a group of unnamed thugs who'd slipped off into the night.

But today, no one was waiting to tackle Gavin at the landing on the second floor. Nothing but a sleepy, quiet, empty office building.

And that door to the locked room, the one that had mysteriously kept power while the rest of the building had been dark, was sitting wide open.

No sound coming from it, no voices or beeps. No light. No smells.

Gavin raised his pistol and approached the door.

Poked his head inside. Whatever power had been

present before was now disconnected, because he was looking at an unused server room, racks of silent machines. Some tables between the server racks, completely devoid of anything. He shined his flashlight over the spaces inside, and it seemed oddly clean. No dust on the tables. He ran a finger across one of the server racks, and it came back clean. The rest of the building had a thin layer of dust coating everything.

Someone had been in this room recently and had made it appear as if it had never been used.

He shined a light at the floor and noticed some scratches near the base of one of the server racks. Kneeling, he traced a finger through the scratches. Someone had moved this rack.

Gavin holstered his weapon and gripped the server rack. With a grunt, he hefted it forward a few inches, took a breath, and then yanked it out another six inches. A coil of wires like intestines stretched out behind it. He shined his light at the wall, at a cutaway section in the exposed drywall.

He wrenched it open and found a slim crawlspace behind the wall. Empty.

"Damn it," he said to the room. "What the hell is going on here?"

He squeezed behind the server rack and reached into the crawlspace. His hand touched something. Small, cylindrical.

Gavin fished the thing out, and he freed himself from

the tight space between the wall and the server rack so he could see the object he was holding.

A ballpoint pen.

With the support of his department, he could have sent this pen off to the lab for fingerprints or DNA. Maybe he could do that anyway, and claim it was for something else. Say he was tracking a fugitive.

But that would be lying. He didn't feel comfortable doing that. With a grunt, he flipped the pen back into the crawlspace and returned everything the way it had been. Stepped back and took another look at this perplexing room. If he'd had his full complement of FBI investigators, he could have had the lab techs sweep the whole room for fingerprints or DNA. But Gavin didn't think he could even call local OKC police. They would run it up the chain and discover that Gavin was a lone wolf here, spinning his wheels across the Midwest.

Gavin ambled down the stairs and paused in the wide-open space of the first floor. Felt the eerie silence of the dark room. None of this made sense. Here, then gone, then here again, and now gone. Who could be doing this?

He left the building and plopped on the step, breathing in the cold air, then letting it exhale as steam. As his eyes drifted up to watch the steam evaporate, he noticed the strangest thing. On a light pole near the building, halfway up, a cluster of security cameras were pointing in all directions. Something about those cameras seemed out of place.

He hustled back to his rental car and dug out the scouting pics from the team that had been following Snoop and had tracked him to this building months ago. Gavin flipped through the black and white exterior photos of the area until he could find one that featured a light pole.

He discovered one pic of that side of the parking lot, showing the same light pole. No cameras on it.

Someone had installed those recently, within the last couple weeks. It had happened after Gavin and Frank had met resistance investigating the building. Why would someone install new security cameras outside an abandoned building?

MICAH SPENT PART of the morning sitting alone in his room, watching a mist of icy rain trickle outside the window. He didn't remember Oklahoma ever being foggy, but a creeping gray cloud had been there when he'd first looked out the window and had slowly engulfed the exterior of the mansion.

As he stared, he considered the clock ticking in the back of his brain. That Snoop would be graduating treatment in a few days, and there had been no real answers.

Nash had already left, having said little to Micah that morning, or in the last few mornings. Nash had acted as a sort of guide when Micah had first arrived, but those days seemed long past. Funny how three weeks in treatment could feel like six months of real-life time.

Micah gave some thought to skipping breakfast and maybe also the morning announcements. He hadn't expected to feel lonely with Frank gone, but he did. Being around people didn't appeal to him today.

Micah flashed back to being sixteen years old, cruising around Tulsa one Saturday afternoon. He'd parked at Utica Square shopping center, about to get lunch, when he'd seen his older brother Kellen sitting on some restaurant's patio with a group of friends. Kellen was supposed to have been away at college, and Micah hadn't known he'd come back into town for the weekend.

When Micah had confronted Kellen about why he'd come back to visit Tulsa without informing his family, Kellen explained that sometimes, you want to see your old friends but not deal with family drama. He'd been staying at a friend's apartment for the weekend.

Micah had been crushed. Disappointed. Took it personally and didn't understand why Kellen had shunned him. Years later, Micah finally understood, and he was able to appreciate that Kellen had truly felt sorry for upsetting him.

Kellen had been a good brother. A much better one than Micah. And now, Micah had a chance to fix it, but he was failing.

As he slid on his jeans, he felt for the severed head of Boba Fett, sitting in his pocket. He slipped out the old bounty hunter and held the plastic piece in his hands.

"Running out of time here, Boba."

Boba Fett said nothing.

"I know what you're going to say. You're going to tell

me I need to go to my morning stuff, even if I don't feel like it. And you're right. But maybe I can just skip announcements? I mean, would anyone actually care if I don't attend?"

Boba Fett remained silent.

"Fine, Boba. I'll go."

Micah shoved the action figure head in his pocket and threw on a shirt and a hoodie. He took one last look at the fog slowly swallowing the bungalows and basketball court, then he left the room.

As he descended the stairs, Micah listened to a familiar voice wafting up from below. The hallway that connected to the mansion branched to the left, and to the right was the bank of payphones.

Micah could now discern the voice. Snoop.

"Listen to me, Rosita," he said. Then, he switched to rapid-fire Spanish, and Micah couldn't understand a word of it. He mentally kicked himself—once again—for not learning more of the language.

Micah slipped down the last few steps, keeping his footfalls light and making sure to remain out of sight of the payphones. He pressed against the wall. Stilled his breathing.

"That's what I've been trying to tell you," Snoop said. "It's a promise. Not like the way things used to be. It's going to be different now. *I'm* going to be different now. But I need you to be a little more patient with me."

Snoop paused, and Micah replayed in his head what he'd heard so far. Sounded like a typical treatment conversation Micah had heard more than once since he'd been here. The recovering alcoholic begging his significant other to take him back, that things would be different this time. But Snoop wasn't currently married and had no girlfriend. His ex-wife was not named Rosita. At least, that's what Frank had said during a recent phone briefing.

"Please, you have to hear me out," Snoop said. "I'm going to set all of this right." Then he dipped back into Spanish, and Micah could only catch random words here and there. Not nearly enough to form any context.

"That's what you keep saying," Snoop said, "but it's not true. I'm doing everything I can. Don't you think I'd be doing everything I can? I want this too. I want this more than I've ever wanted anything." He paused for a few seconds. "I think about that every day. And I know it's taken a long time. *Seis mas dias.*"

Micah had understood that phrase. Six more days. He did the math in his head. Six days from now would be Snoop's last day in treatment, the day he was scheduled to board a plane to Vietnam.

"Just a few more days, Rosita. Hold on a little bit longer, and then it will all be over."

DAY 23.1

HENRIETTA DRYDEN'S PULSE hadn't been at a normal level all day. She'd rescheduled her morning sessions so she could have some alone time to think and pace and do some laps around this spacious mansion she occupied for eight hours a day. Wasn't working to ease her nerves. The present felt like the past, and that was a horrible place to be.

The things she wanted to forget. The lies and the heartbreak. The divorce. The children. A promising political career torn to pieces. The affair that wasn't actually an affair. If the public only knew what had actually happened, they wouldn't have let her slide with a simple resignation and a few cruel memes shared around the internet.

She walked the halls of The Stone, a magnificent building with an endless amount of history. She ambled up the hallway from the dorms to the main building and entered Little Library. She'd once caught some patients having a threesome, right here in this public room. The three had stayed back during dinner time, and they were all naked and writhing together when Dryden came strolling through. With a gasp, she'd dropped her mug of tea onto the floor as the three lovers scrambled to get back into their clothes.

Next, she entered the Cornerstone main lobby, with the stairs up to the counselors' offices and the stairs down to the basement. Across from that, the nurses' station and the door to the recovery suite. In this very room, she'd seen one patient try to strangle another patient to death. Two men fighting, something about a woman they both liked. Dryden had known the object of their affection, and the woman in question had been playing them off each other to achieve maximum attention.

Dryden had experienced a few good years here at The Stone. Sometimes more bad than good, but she liked to think that she'd helped a portion of her patients outright, and for others, she'd planted a seed that would later sprout into the desire to work for lasting sobriety. She tried not to think about the vast collection of unclaimed coffee mugs in the attic; all those former patients who couldn't stay sober for a full year to come back and receive the ones they'd painted.

A year was an eternity. Henrietta Dryden knew that fact well.

She needed to end these distractions. Needed to

focus. She returned to her office, sat at her desk, and flipped through the treatment plan pile until she landed on Micah T.'s chart. Back to their earlier sessions, when he'd actually talked to her. Over the last few, he'd said less and less. He'd stopped being argumentative, had given the impression of being a model patient. Agreed with whatever she said.

Dryden hadn't believed his act for a second.

And since he was only here five more days, they had one final session together before she would have no choice but to graduate him. Micah's Hot Seat group was tomorrow, one of the last rites of passage for patients.

He would fly through here untouched unless she could find something concrete.

On the first page of his session history, she discovered a note about him being a professor at Tulsa Community College. But, he wouldn't say what he taught.

Dryden opened her laptop and navigated to the TCC website, then clicked on the faculty link. She scrolled down the page, picture after picture and bio after bio. Reading about English professors, Psychology professors, Philosophy professors, but no Micah.

She thought she'd maybe missed it, so she tapped *Control-F* and searched for his first name. Nothing. There was no Micah Templeton on this page at all.

She scrolled to the bottom of the website and found the contact info for the TCC administrator's office. Dialed.

"Tulsa Community College, how can I help you?"

"Yes," Dryden said, "my name is Henrietta James, and I work at the Chicago Sun-Times. We received a letter to the editor from one of your professors, a Mr. Micah Templeton? I just want to confirm his position at your college before we publish his letter."

"One moment, ma'am. I'll get you that information."

Hold music clicked on, some smooth jazz saxophone tune. Dryden drummed her nails against the desk while she waited. The clock on the wall ticked, a gentle pouring sound of the water in her fish tank gave her the slightest need to pee.

The line clicked back on. "Ma'am, did you say Micah Templeton?"

"I did."

"Are you positive about that last name?"

"I am."

"Then I'm afraid we don't have anyone on the faculty by that name. Did you try Oklahoma City Community College? Sometimes people get us and *oh-triple-see* mixed up. I can give you their number if you like."

"That must be it," Dryden said. "My mistake. Thank you for your time."

Dryden ended the call as she gripped Micah's session notes, crinkling the edges of the paper.

~

Gavin Belmont paced his motel room in Oklahoma City, waiting for a phone call. The phone sat on the bedspread, and he glanced at it each time he completed another lap of the room.

His belly rumbled, so he grabbed the phone and his room key, then shut the door behind him. He paced down the carpeted hallway until he found a vending machine near the elevator. Junk food, mostly.

Gavin missed his wife's cooking. While her family had been strongly Germanic in origin, his wife made the best Italian food he'd ever tasted in his entire life. Chicken cacciatore, lasagna, manicotti… she could do it all. The only nearby Italian restaurant that rated above three stars on the online rating websites was Olive Garden, and Gavin wasn't inclined to give that a whirl.

He had to believe what he was doing here had enough merit to miss his wife's cooking for more than three weeks straight. To pause the nightly pre-bed installments of Harry Potter and the Sorcerer's Stone he'd shared with his two children.

With a sigh, he swiped his card and punched the N3 button. The coil unfurled and dropped a package of potato chips to the bottom. He sauntered back down the hall, defeated, as he opened the bag and plopped a chip in his mouth.

Finally, after waiting all day, the phone rang. He quickly opened the door and dropped the chips on the counter inside the room.

Gavin thumbed the *accept* button. "Hello?"

"Mr. Belmont? This is Jarrod from SafeZone. Sorry it's taken me so long to get back to you. We had an electrical issue down in Moore we've been dealing with the last couple days."

"No problem. I need to ask you a couple questions if that's okay."

"Go right ahead, buddy. I'm all ears."

"Your company provides security for the Pine Ridge office park on Southwest 89th?"

"You heard that right. We certainly do provide the cameras and maintenance at that location. Or, we did in the past, would be the most accurate way to say that. We don't have much to do there besides the occasional drive-by. Anyway, what can I do for you, sir?"

"I'm interested to know about a bank of security cameras that were installed there sometime in the last few days. A cluster of them on a light pole at the north end of the parking lot."

"Uhh, I'm not sure what you're referring to, Mr. Belmont. We don't have any cameras at that location."

Gavin gripped the phone. It was the answer he'd been expecting, but it instilled a sour taste in his mouth, regardless. "But if there were cameras there, your company would have been the ones to install them, correct?"

"Certainly, sir. Security companies are competitive as can be, and if someone had stepped on our toes like that, we'd know about it. All that said, we haven't had active security monitoring at that site for more than a year. We haven't authorized resuming any level of surveillance. I can assure you that."

"Okay, Jarrod. Thanks for your time."

Gavin tapped the button to end the call and dropped his phone back onto the bed. The obvious answer was that whoever had attacked Gavin and Frank that night had installed the cameras after clearing out of the building.

But why? And who the hell was it?

WHILE ALL THE patients and staff were at lunch, Dryden ventured out of her office, toward the dorms attached to the mansion's south side. Micah's room was on the second floor.

He was obviously not who he'd claimed to be. At a place like Cornerstone, that invariably meant one thing: he was moving product through the treatment center. Drugs, or some other contraband.

As Dryden reached the end of the hallway, Rhonda Delaney, Cornerstone's executive director, was slinking down the stairs. Rhonda was wearing tight jeans and a muted brown top. Not exactly the most professional outfit, but Dryden supposed the director could wear whatever she wanted.

"Afternoon, Henrietta."

Dryden had no desire to halt her investigation, but

when the boss wants to talk, you don't have much choice. "Hi, ma'am."

"How is your schedule today?"

Dryden looked up the stairs, itching to get on with her task. The patients would sometimes come back from lunch early. "Light, I suppose?"

"Excellent. We need to take advantage of the easy days, whenever the chance presents itself."

"Very true."

Rhonda's face changed, adopting that pained look Dryden knew all too well. The director usually wore it when she was about to hand out discipline. "I hope you know that you're a valued member of my staff. I've been thrilled you've been a part of the team since you joined us."

Dryden smiled and nodded, waiting for a *but*. "I appreciate the sentiment, Rhonda."

"It's important that we present a united front. I don't like to think of it as *us vs. the patients*, but it can feel that way sometimes."

"I understand."

Rhonda clapped her hands together. "Excellent. Well, I'm glad we had a chance to chat, and I'll let you get back to your 'light' day."

Rhonda dipped her head and shoulders, almost like a slight bow, and then passed Dryden on the stairs. She disappeared around the bend, back up the hallway toward the mansion proper.

What an odd exchange. Rhonda wasn't usually so

cryptic, but things at The Stone had definitely not been usual lately. Dryden shrugged it off and continued up the stairs, pausing outside of the second room on the left.

She opened the room he shared with Nash, the cowboy pillhead. For a moment, she stood in the middle of a messy room, debating if she wanted to go through the whole rigamarole of removing dresser drawers and pulling up mattresses. Protocol said she should have a nurse with her, but that was a bad option. Oscar was the nurse on duty, and that burly Native American with the moles on his face had never liked Dryden. He hadn't been in her corner, not even once.

How deep should she search?

She ignored the easy spots. Micah wouldn't have stashed drugs in a drawer or anything else as obvious as that. She slipped a keycard from her pocket and knelt in front of an electrical outlet. She used the hard plastic edge to remove the screws, then pulled the socket back and peered around. Nothing. She put it back in place and then checked the other three outlets, with the same result.

Micah seemed more clever than using electrical sockets.

Curiosity tugged at her, and she felt the itch to look through Micah's personal things, even though she knew she wouldn't find drugs hidden in his underwear.

She started with his dressers, looking through his scant collection of clothes. Jeans, t-shirts, a few hooded sweatshirts. While some patients wore slacks and dress shirts to distance themselves from the former lives they'd led, Micah didn't look like the kind of person who even knew how to tie a tie.

Next, she explored the nightstand by his bed. A scarred-up paperback sat on his nightstand next to a collection of quarters, probably for laundry. Interestingly, he had a lack of framed pictures placed around it. Unusual.

Inside the nightstand, Dryden found a container of breath mints, a pen, and a notepad. She flipped open the notepad to the first page and read.

Bob D - Dec 19th - Anger lecture
Anger is an acid that can do more harm to the vessel in which it is stored than to anything on which it is poured.

She flipped pages and found more lecture notes like this. A few pages had doodles. Mostly pictures of guitars or people playing guitars. Some pages had song lyrics scrawled in the corners. None of it was useful.

Dryden checked the time on her phone. Lunch would be over soon. Where would a devious person like Micah hide his drugs?

The ceiling panels caught her eye, and so she dragged a chair into the center of the room. She stood on it and pushed a panel up and then over, but she wasn't tall enough to see above the panels. With one foot on the back of the chair, she leaped up and latched onto a pipe, barely managing to grasp it.

Below her, the chair tipped over and toppled to the floor. She was suspended, her feet dangling in the air below her.

"Shit."

She tightened her grip on the pipe. Felt a moment of gratitude that it wasn't a hot water pipe. With her free hand, she lifted her phone and hit the flashlight app. She swung her hand around until she found exactly what she was looking for: a small backpack, nestled above the ceiling panels. She stuck the phone between her teeth to free up a hand and snatched at the backpack, but then she noticed the strangest thing: the ceiling above had lines in it. A rectangular cut-out.

A trap door.

Dryden retrieved the backpack and looked down at the drop below her. Good thing she wasn't in heels today.

She let go and plummeted to the floor, sending a painful jolt up through her heels, dissipating into her calves. She groaned against the pain but didn't feel any lasting damage when she tested each foot.

Dryden opened the pack and found a collection of all sorts of forbidden goodies inside. Pills. Weed. White powder that was probably cocaine.

"Got you, you son of a bitch," she said.

Instinct told her to take this straight to Rhonda, but she paused for a moment. Finding this bag up here didn't prove anything. He'd never walked around campus with it. There was nothing inside that tied it to Micah, and finding it in the space above his room wasn't conclusive. He could simply say he didn't know it had been there. Some former patient had left it.

Maybe she needed to catch him in the act.

And what about that trap door? Who was above this room?

She threw the backpack back up through the hole and replaced the ceiling panel. Returned the chair to the desk and left the room.

Dryden climbed the stairs to the third floor and opened the room right above Micah's. A female room, judging by the bra hanging over the back of a chair.

Her mouth dropped open when she saw a notebook on the desk with a name scrawled on the front: *Leighton*.

This explained so much. Why the young woman had followed Micah around like a streamer attached to a parade float. Why she'd stabbed him with the scissors. It wasn't a lovers' quarrel, it had been a disagreement among coworkers.

The pieces were coming together. With a little care, she could spin this into something concrete.

Now, Dryden knew for sure that she needed to keep this to herself. She had to observe both Micah and Leighton to catch them red-handed. If she did that, she could take it to the Cornerstone director, and she would be made Assistant Director for sure. From there, she was a heartbeat away from running this place.

DAY 24.1

MICAH COULDN'T DECIDE what to do with his hands. He tried resting them on his knees, but that felt awkward. He tried shoving them in his pockets, which also seemed strange. Sitting in this circle with exactly half of The Stone's patients around him, all of them staring, nothing he could do would make him comfortable for his Hot Seat.

He didn't want to be here, but this was part of the game. And, as uncomfortable as he was, it was a momentary distraction from the fact that he had four days left to solve all his problems, and he still had no good answers.

Hot Seat was a rite of passage that patients in their fourth week had to endure. At the morning announcements, all patients received two slips of paper. On one slip, they were to write an *asset* for their group's Hot Seat participant on that given day. On the other slip, every patient would write a *liability*. A positive and a negative.

Then, in the afternoon, Group A patients gathered in one room, and Group B patients in another. They would line the edges of each room as the Hot Seat person sat in a chair in the middle of the circle, and the counselor would read the patient's assets and liabilities in front of all of them. Like a communal inventory.

Micah had joined his group to watch one of these almost every afternoon since he'd been here. Seemed like a terribly nerve-wracking experience. Some of the patients' liabilities cut right to the person's core, brought them to tears. During yesterday's Hot Seat, the counselor had only read the patient's assets, because that particular person was so good at beating up on herself, the counselor had said she didn't need any more ammunition.

Micah didn't expect Dryden to let him off so easily.

In his Hot Seat, Dryden read through each item with a hint of malice on her face. She had grown more and more suspicious and hostile toward Micah as the days wore on. Didn't matter, though, he only had to withstand four more days of her sideways glances.

Dryden had read all of the assets first, which was unusual. Counselors usually kept the positive stuff for the end. Not Dryden. As she read each one, Micah felt the eyes of the community probing him. Nash was here, Leighton was here, as were thirty others, many of them only having been residents for a few days.

Micah's assets were largely critiques related to his reaction to the stabbing. They lauded his bravery for coming back to treatment after that horrible episode.

They praised his positive attitude while he was recovering from the injury. His courage for not skipping lectures and classes. Micah wasn't surprised to hear such generic assets in the list.

He didn't listen too carefully, anyway. He had drifted off, worrying about his brother. Worrying about what would happen if Micah couldn't somehow still pull this off. He kept picturing Kellen and his family, living out of their car. Their lives wrecked.

Micah had to do something. He had to fix this.

When Dryden finished the assets, she paused, drew in a harsh breath, and turned the page.

His liabilities list was predictable; most of the items mentioned that he was quiet, didn't open up to people, seemed to withdraw and didn't make friends. They warned of isolation as a relapse trigger, something that real-life Micah Reed knew all too well.

Micah spends too much time alone, reading and not talking to people.

Micah goes off by himself a lot, wandering out in the woods behind the mansion.

Micah doesn't like to talk about himself. I asked him a question about his hometown, and he just stared at me.

Micah T. doesn't get to know people. Not reaching out to people can cost you your life.

Micah had to listen with a filter on. He knew he was playing a part at The Stone. But, some of these things in the list were absolutely true. Micah had never been good with people.

Dryden read off the list slowly, one at a time, giving each predictable item the same intonation as the last. But one liability was different. When she came to it, she paused. Her lips curled into a frown as if she was considering whether or not to read it.

Eventually, she said, "Micah likes to stick his nose where it doesn't belong. Someday, that's going to get him hurt."

A few heads turned, and a low rumble of whispers fluttered around the room. It was an odd thing to say in the Hot Seat. Both vague and specific at the same time.

But Micah knew exactly what it meant.

He scanned the room, checking the faces of each person for some reaction. He landed on Nash, his roommate, the confrontational ex-cowboy.

And Nash held Micah's eye contact, a scowl on his face.

PATIENTS ALWAYS HAD a free period baked into their schedules after a Hot Seat. To wander the grounds and internalize the lessons learned. Micah, though, didn't need to wander to find himself. He was concerned with only one item in the list: the cryptic warning about sticking his nose where it didn't belong.

And the look Nash had given him which implied he'd been the one who'd written that comment.

Micah didn't know what to make of Nash. So far, Micah had suspected him of being the smallpox buyer, the seller, and also of having nothing to do with it. Maybe Snoop had told the truth that there was no smallpox here, but Nash and Snoop had to be connected to all this, somehow.

Micah slumped in one of the chairs in the lobby, debating if he wanted to go for a walk. While he was thinking, Nash bounded down the stairs, oblivious to

Micah's presence. Nash turned left, straight for the front doors. Micah rose from his chair and followed.

Micah waited a full five seconds after his roommate had gone out the front before opening the door after him. Nash was in the parking lot, shuffling gravel as he marched toward the main entrance. He took a can of Skoal from his pocket, thumped it a few times with his thumb, then plopped a plug of tobacco into his mouth. Spit a big glob of brown juice on the hood of a car.

Micah was about to descend the front steps when the door opened behind him, and there stood nurse Oscar, shivering in short-sleeve scrubs.

"Hey Micah, got a second?"

Nash slipped beyond the front entrance, and Micah noticed Oscar's eyes also tracking Nash. "Sure, Oscar."

Oscar pointed to the steps, and they both sat.

"Hot Seat today, huh?" Oscar said.

"Yep."

"It can be brutal. Believe me, I know."

"How do you know?"

"I'm a graduate, myself. Been sober six years."

Micah almost replied that he had fifteen months, but he stopped himself at the last second. "Wow," he said instead.

Oscar grinned. "It's not as impressive as it sounds. Just like you, I do it one day at a time. How is your side feeling?"

"Much better. Almost no pain at all."

"Good, good. If you need extra Tylenol or anything,

you know you can come to us, right? Anytime, day or night."

Micah got the feeling that Oscar was working up to a point, so he nodded and waited for the nurse to continue.

Oscar grimaced. "Since your injury, have you been approached by anyone? Reporters, bloggers, anybody like that?"

"No, not at all. I talked to the cops at the hospital, but haven't heard a peep since then."

"Oh, okay."

"Why do you ask, Oscar?"

He shook his head. "Just curious, that's all." Oscar patted Micah on the knee a couple times. "Well, I'll bet you want a little time alone after your Hot Seat. Mine knocked me for a loop, for sure, but it's one of the best things that ever happened to me."

"Thanks," Micah said, and then the big guy lumbered to his feet to shuffle back inside the building. All conversations with Oscar seemed to go like this.

Micah had now lost sight of Nash, so he gave up following him and returned to the building. He checked the public schedule posted near the nurses' station. B group, which was Snoop's group, was in the basement now, painting their coffee mugs. Micah descended the stairs to find Snoop wearing a paint-stained apron, hunched over a table. Brush in one hand. The cup in front of him had been painted with black and red stripes.

"Snoop," Micah said, and Snoop set down his brush.

He didn't answer, only stared. Micah realized he may have entered a little too forcefully, as half the room had stopped what they were doing to gawk at him.

"Going with a death-metal theme for your cup?" Micah said, motioning at the darkly-painted thing.

"What?"

"Nothing. Can we talk in private?"

Snoop sighed and removed his apron, then he tilted his head toward the adjoining laundry room. Micah left, and Snoop followed.

Industrial-sized washers and dryers lined floor-to-ceiling in this space that stank of dryer sheets and sour water. An older man was standing in front of a dryer, shaking out a pair of white boxers.

Snoop cleared his throat. "Scram."

"Sorry," Micah said to the man. "Can you give us a few minutes?"

The old guy shrugged, dropped his underwear into a basket, and left the room.

Once they were alone, Snoop leaned against a folding table. "Why you storming into the basement like that, white boy?"

"Nash, my roommate."

"Yep?"

"Did you know him before this? Have you had any contact with him at all before?"

Snoop crossed his arms and flicked a thumb under his chin a couple times. "Nope. Why you ask?"

"Is he maybe from the Dos Cruces cartel, or someone you had business with before?"

"He ain't Dos Cruces. I would know if he was from my old crew. We weren't global like your old buddies. Small, loyal, independent. And I never done business with him outside of that, either. He's shady as fuck. I don't keep people like that around me."

Micah removed the folded Hot Seat printout from his back pocket. He opened it to the liabilities page and pointed at the comment about sticking his nose where it didn't belong.

Snoop whistled. "That's harsh. You think Nash wrote that?"

"Well, it wasn't you, was it?"

As soon as Micah had asked, he realized Snoop wouldn't have even filled out Hot Seat slips for him. Snoop was in a different "group" so he'd attended a different Hot Seat.

"No," Snoop said, "you and me are good. What about Leighton? I mean, the bitch did stab you with a pair of scissors. Someone who'd do that might hold a grudge, know what I'm saying?"

Micah studied the page and considered it, but that theory didn't add up. Leighton had ignored him for the last week or so, ever since she'd found a boyfriend to occupy her time. "It's not her."

"Sorry, Micah," Snoop said, shrugging. "I don't know what to tell you."

Micah folded the printout and shoved it back into his

pocket. "Okay. Thanks, Snoop. Sorry to pull you away from cup-painting."

Micah felt the itch to ask Snoop about the phone call the other day, about Rosita. Who she was, what they'd been talking about. What, exactly, was going to happen in four more days. But, he couldn't let the former cartel member know he'd overheard that conversation. He'd already checked with Frank, and there was no way to retrieve the conversation from phone records. Not without court orders, and that would take weeks or months.

Micah turned to leave, but Snoop held up a hand. "Wait."

"Yes?"

Snoop opened his mouth to speak, then he stopped himself. The corners of his mouth pulled down. He was trembling.

"What's going on, Snoop?"

Snoop gritted his teeth and then snapped his mouth shut. "Nothing. I have to get back to painting my cup."

And with that, Snoop strutted out of the room, brushing past Micah.

DAY 25.1

DRYDEN HATED THE daily staff meetings, only slightly more than she hated doing announcements. The only good thing about announcements was that it allowed her to skip the staff meetings, so she didn't mind when her turn came up in the rotation.

This morning wasn't one of those mornings, so she was stuck in the staff meeting with the Cornerstone director Rhonda, Oscar the nurse, and a half dozen counselors. None of them wanted to be here, either. That's what Dryden assumed.

They would discuss disciplines to be handed out, work assignment duties, troubled patients. Leighton was often a topic of discussion. She and her boyfriend and their displays of public affection constantly placed them on the verge of being kicked out. Obviously, she and that longhaired guy had been sneaking off somewhere to bump uglies, but no one had been able to prove it yet.

But the fact that she had stabbed another patient with a pair of scissors? No, that they couldn't talk about.

And Micah. He was such a model patient, none of the staff could ever pin anything on him. Not dealing drugs, not sneaking out for who-knows-what shady meetings in the woods, nothing. But Dryden would have a surprise for all of them, as soon as she could link him to the backpack she'd found hidden above his ceiling tiles.

"I know we haven't discussed this in a while," Rhonda said, "but we need to start thinking again about the variable treatment schedule."

The counselors collectively groaned, and Rhonda raised a hand to call for silence. "I know, I know, but the landscape of what health insurance will pay for has changed, and it's going to continue to change. We can be prepared for it, or we can keep treading water."

"Ain't like it used to be," said crusty old Counselor Bob.

"That's for sure, Bob," Rhonda said. "I'll add it to New Business for tomorrow's meeting. Next, we need to talk about patient of the week. I'll take nominations if you have anyone to suggest."

"I would like to nominate Micah T.," Oscar said.

"Good one," said another counselor.

Dryden sat up straight. Couldn't believe what she was hearing. All around the room, the heads nodded at the suggestion, as if Micah were the kind of person to be rewarded for his behavior. The sort of patient the others should emulate.

Director Rhonda clicked her pen and made some notes. "I like it. He had his Hot Seat yesterday, I believe. Right, Henrietta?"

For a moment, Dryden couldn't speak. She was too astonished at the notion.

"I think he's handled himself well after everything that's happened to him," Rhonda said. "Are there no other nominations?"

Dryden threw up her hands. "Are you people kidding me? Micah's one of the most dishonest, manipulative patients we've ever had."

Everyone around the table stared. Dryden felt the room grow smaller. The staff meetings were usually so tame and rote, her sudden elevation of tone had shocked the room into silence.

"What are you talking about?" Bob said.

"Well," Rhonda said, "you are his counselor, Henrietta. If you have something you want to add to the discussion, I'm willing to hear it. Nothing is set in stone yet."

"He's been dealing drugs," Dryden blurted, and instantly regretted it. Without even thinking, she'd played her ace, with no idea where she was supposed to go next.

"That's a serious accusation," Rhonda said. "Do you have any proof of this?"

Dryden sat back and wiped a hand across her face. That had been such a stupid move, and one she couldn't now retract. She had no choice but to spill the rest of it. "He lied about his job. Said he was a professor at TCC, but they have no record of him."

"What does that have to do with selling drugs?" Oscar said.

Dryden seethed at the chubby man. "I'm getting to that, Nurse Oscar. There's a backpack in the ceiling tiles above his room, filled with all kinds of nasty things."

"This backpack is there right now in his room?" Rhonda said. "You know this, and you didn't confiscate it?"

Dryden stumbled over her words. "It's complicated."

Rhonda pointed at Oscar. "Go now and check, please. We will hold the meeting until this is settled."

"Wait," Dryden said as she jumped up from her chair. "He's my patient. I'm going with you."

And with that, the drug-hunting party left the room.

MICAH KEPT HIS distance but made sure Snoop didn't get too far ahead of him. Since Snoop's strange, aborted declaration in the laundry room yesterday, Micah couldn't help thinking Snoop knew things he wasn't telling. Snoop feared something or had a secret.

Or maybe the pain on Snoop's face was only part of his personality. Every day, Micah felt like he was seeing a different person hiding behind those icy, black eyes.

And only three days remained.

There was the Snoop who warned this *white boy* to stay away from him. A different Snoop told him brutally personal secrets, like his failed suicide attempt. Another Snoop sneered when Dos Cruces came into the conversation. And yet another Snoop was on the phone, begging this mystery woman Rosita to give him another chance, the pain in his voice threatening to give way to tears.

Micah paid careful attention to the sticks on the ground so he wouldn't snap one and give himself away as he trailed Snoop through the forest behind Cornerstone. He'd been lucky so far that Snoop hadn't turned to check behind him. Micah skirted from tree to tree, pausing at each one to let Snoop gain some distance between them.

In the handful of times Micah had explored the woods back here, he'd only found two items of interest: a wooden box filled with various injection paraphernalia, and a backpack stocked with *Hustler* magazines and whiskey. Despite Snoop's claims of how seriously he was taking his sobriety, maybe he was out here hunting for something like that.

But Micah knew they'd already passed the tree where he'd recovered the backpack, so Snoop wasn't headed in that direction. But the box? If Snoop was still using, that might explain the mood swings.

And part of Micah hoped whatever Snoop was doing out here, he wasn't going to get high. That Micah would feel terribly disappointed in his frenemy Snoop if he hadn't been serious about sobriety. Like losing a fellow soldier on the battlefield.

And then Snoop stopped and sat on a downed log at the edge of a clearing. This time, he did turn to check behind him, and Micah managed to leap to a tree to cover himself. A murmur of pain pulsed in Micah's side, but not nearly as bad as it had hurt a few days ago.

Micah peered around the tree at Snoop, sitting there, staring off into space. Hands folded in his lap, shoulders slumped. Maybe he'd come here to think. Or maybe he was waiting for some sign.

Five full minutes elapsed with Snoop staring off into the spiderweb of tree branches above him, Micah sheltered behind the thick trunk of a pecan tree, shivering, waiting for something to happen. Five minutes of silent anticipation that felt like an eternity.

Micah was readying himself to give up and return to the mansion. Then, from a cluster of trees on the left emerged a man wearing a long black coat, with a thick scarf draped around his neck and a baseball cap pulled low to hide his features. Gloves on his hands and large sunglasses. Micah could see no part of this man except for a chunk of black hair jutting from the back of the cap. Like a mummy.

The man sat on the log next to Snoop, and they turned to face each other. Micah again wished for some super spy equipment so he could remotely eavesdrop to their conversation. But no, he didn't even have his phone.

For a long time—maybe twenty or thirty seconds— they simply stared at each other. Like two boxers at a weigh-in, trying to use intimidation to get into each others' heads.

What was this?

Then, Snoop broke the silence. As he and the stranger talked, they each began gesturing with their hands. The conversation became more animated. The hand motions grew larger and more aggressive. Snoop stood, and the man stood, and Snoop pushed the man. The man pushed back. Snoop raised a fist, threatening to punch. The other man held up his hands in surrender.

Another pause, and they both seemed frozen. Breathing, waiting for the next shift in action to happen.

Snoop lowered his fist, and they shook hands. What the hell had they been talking about?

And then, the man patted Snoop on the shoulder and turned back into the forest. Micah had to make a decision. He figured Snoop would return to The Stone, so he had to find out where this stranger was going. Maybe this was the same man who Micah and Frank had chased off last week.

Micah cut left in a wide berth around the trees so Snoop wouldn't see him. Snoop was still sitting on that log, staring off into space.

Micah stayed low, moving from tree to tree, eyes on Snoop. If the former cartel member saw him, Micah would eradicate any trust he'd built up so far.

Snoop didn't budge.

Once Micah was shrouded by the forest and out of Snoop's range of vision, he broke into a run in the direction the stranger had gone.

And when he reached the area he'd last seen the man, nothing but unpopulated forest looked back at Micah. The stranger had disappeared.

DAY 25.3

FTER THE REVELATION in the staff meeting, Dryden marched through the mansion, with Oscar and two of his nurses in tow. She felt a bit like a conquering warrior, striding across the battle to receive the enemy's surrender. If only she had a cape dragging behind her.

Patients in the hallways stopped what they were doing to watch Dryden and her crew sweep through the little library, toward the dorms. While no one in here ever endured anything like the prison cell-tossings she'd seen on TV shows, the patients knew that the staff usually ferreted out any contraband. And they recognized a search party when they saw it.

Dryden ascended the stairs to the second floor and threw back the door to Micah's room. His shirtless roommate Nash was on the bed, reclining, reading a magazine.

"What's going on?" Nash said.

"Out," Dryden said. "You can't be in here right now."

Nash attempted to protest, but Oscar stood over him, his large frame blocking him from Dryden's vision. "Come on, Nash. We need you out of here."

"I feel like if y'all are going to search my room, I have a right to be here. This is still America, ain't it? Do I waive my rights just because I'm a patient here?"

"Out," Oscar said. "I'm not going to say it again." He didn't ball his fists or flex his muscles, but the bulky nurse stood his ground. He even seemed to grow a little larger, like a puffer fish.

For a moment, Dryden thought Nash wasn't going to back down, either. The former rodeo star narrowed his eyes and breathed, his naked chest rising and falling.

Finally, Nash jumped to his feet, grabbed a sweatshirt, and limped out of the room in a huff. Dryden shut the door behind her. Oscar and his nurses donned latex gloves.

"There," she said as she pointed at the tile she'd removed before. One of the nurses scooted a chair underneath it, and Oscar climbed on top, removed the tile, and leaned up onto his tiptoes to elevate his head above the tiles.

He held up a pen light. Swished it around.

Oscar coughed as some dust settled through the ceiling tile hole. "Can't see much up here. I'm looking for a backpack?"

"Yes," Dryden said. "A green backpack. It was a little ways off to the side, maybe two tiles over."

"There's nothing up here but cobwebs and mouse poop."

A chill trickled down the back of Dryden's neck. "What? That can't be. Let me up there."

Oscar ducked down and clicked off his pen light. "Ms. Dryden, there's no contraband up here. I'm sorry."

"It's not possible." She stormed to the chair and pointed at the floor, trying to tell Oscar to get down.

He shook his head. "I can't let you up here, Ms. Dryden. You might fall and hurt yourself. I can barely reach up here, as it is."

"Get down, nurse. I'm going to look for myself."

"I'm afraid I can't let you do that."

"Fuck," she said as she stormed out of the room. It's not as if she could wrestle Oscar to the ground and leap into the hole.

She'd had a chance to use this backpack as leverage, and now she'd blown it. With all of the other pressure weighing down on her at this moment, why couldn't she be allowed this one little victory? Huh? Why couldn't the universe grant her this one simple request?

As she marched down the stairs, she saw Micah standing at the bank of payphones, receiver in one hand, and a quarter in the other.

He replaced the receiver back into the cradle. "What's going on up there? Were you in my room?"

"You listen to me," she hissed at him, "you think

you're so damn clever."

"Ms. Dryden, I don't know what—"

"Shut up, Micah, just shut up."

"No," he said. "I'm not going to shut up. I'm tired of you treating me like a criminal. You're always talking about rigorous honesty and how secrets make you sick, but isn't it time *you* got honest?"

"I have no idea what you're talking about."

"What happened to the scissors, Ms. Dryden?"

"What?"

"The scissors from my… accident. Why weren't the police able to find them?"

The words hit her like a semi truck. Micah was accusing *her* of covering up the stabbing. Of all the things in the universe that could have occurred, she would have never predicted this one.

For a few seconds, she couldn't clear her head to think of a response.

When the fog lifted and the surprise faded, Dryden knew exactly why the scissors had never been found. Rhonda Delaney, Cornerstone's director, had to have recovered the scissors that night and dealt with it. Rhonda would value Cornerstone's precious standing in the treatment community over the truth.

But, of course, Dryden couldn't admit that to Micah.

"Got nothing to say?" he said.

She resisted the urge to give in and continue the war of words. Instead, she pursed her lips and rushed away from him, feeling her temperature rise to a boiling point.

DAY 26.1

FRANK SIGHED AS Gavin pulled into the abandoned office building parking lot, yet again. Time after time they'd come here, found nothing, only to return a couple days later. Doing the same thing over and over again, but expecting a different result each time. Frank was tired of sleeping in motel beds. Tired of losing business back in Denver by keeping Mueller Bail Enforcement closed indefinitely.

"We going inside this time?" Frank said.

Gavin pointed up at a light pole, to a collection of security cameras clustered near the top.

"I see them," Frank said.

"Look brand new, don't they?"

Frank nodded, waited for Gavin to continue.

"The security company didn't install them. This came from somebody else."

"You have a theory, I assume?"

"I do," Gavin said. "When the deal is done, this is where they're bringing the smallpox to process it. To ready it for shipment. What we stumbled on a couple weeks ago when we were attacked? That was preliminary work to get the room ready."

"But they'd cleared it all out by the next time you came back. That doesn't make a whole lotta sense."

"Maybe they felt the heat. Maybe they'd finished staging what they needed to do. Either way, this building is important. I can feel it in my bones, Frank. They are going to come back here again."

Frank watched a raccoon skittering through some shrubs across the parking lot. It reared up on its hind legs, chewing something. Just as quickly as it had come, the beast dashed away, past the parking lot.

He shifted in his seat. "What you can't seem to answer, though, is who the 'they' is in all this."

"Cartel. Has to be. Snoop double-crossed the cartel, and now they're going to steal back their smallpox. They get it from him, they bring it here, transfer it to some new container, and then they sell it to a third party. Maybe this staging area is to split it up into smaller chunks to sell it to multiple buyers."

Frank wanted to believe his friend. Wanted to continue being supportive, but almost a month had elapsed since they'd met here in Oklahoma, and the scenario kept getting harder and harder to believe. Frank wondered if staying close to Micah might not be a better use of his time. Whether this smallpox existed or not, Micah was in deep over there at Cornerstone, an inch away from a very dangerous individual. Not to mention the stabbing and the counselor who was continually breathing down his neck. The more Frank thought about Micah's situation, the less he liked it.

"I don't know, Gavin. It all seems to be based on smoke and mirrors."

Gavin's phone beeped and he fished it from his pocket. "One sec," he said, his eyes widening at the screen. "This could be good news."

Frank waved a hand to give permission.

"Tommy? How's it going?" Gavin paused, then chuckled a little. "Well, that's what you get for being a Ravens fan." He nodded a few times, listening. "Uh-huh. Uh-huh. That's fantastic. So I'll meet them at the airport?" He paused again, nodding. "You have no idea how much this means to me. Right. Right. I'll take good care of them, trust me."

Gavin ended the call and gritted his teeth while he smiled. Pumped his fist in the air, almost bumping up against the steering wheel.

"What was that about?" Frank said.

"Buddy of mine in the FBI is going to lend me some tactical agents from Houston. They're HRT and apparently sitting around, doing nothing, and somehow under-budget. It's a perfect storm. They're coming tomorrow."

"Okay, but I don't see how that helps us. You still

don't know what to do with them when they get here."

"Doesn't matter," Gavin said, shaking his head. "It's all going to be good now. The cavalry is coming."

ICAH HAD AVOIDED Dryden for the rest of the day yesterday, after her fierce words by the payphones. Confronting her about the scissors had been an impulsive move, and one that wouldn't have worked out to his advantage, no matter her response. It's not as if Micah *wanted* the scissors to be recovered. But, in the moment, he'd wanted to see Dryden sweat. To finally see her flustered.

And it had worked, so much so that Micah became convinced she'd had nothing to do with covering up the attack in the hallway. And it didn't matter, anyway. The cops hadn't been back, Micah hadn't been bothered by anyone else regarding the incident. Better left in the dark.

He'd heard through the grapevine that she and Oscar had searched his room and come up empty. Expecting to find drugs, most likely. Micah himself had also conducted a search of the room, looking for drugs, not long after moving into The Stone. He hadn't found anything then, either.

But what weighed the heaviest on Micah's mind today wasn't paranoid Henrietta Dryden. It was Snoop Jiménez. Micah believed Snoop when he said he had nothing to do with the smallpox, and that he was here to get sober. But then there was that strange, aborted admission in the laundry room. The conversation with "Rosita" on the payphone. The even stranger argument with the mysterious visitor back in the woods.

Snoop wasn't telling the whole story. And Micah had only two days left to figure out the truth.

After lunch, Micah set out to find him. Another patient said he'd seen Snoop and some others disappear into the chapel to work on their Wish Boxes. The Wish Box was another treatment staple, during which, patients wrote down one fear and one hope on separate slips of paper. The hope went into the wish box, to be buried in a hole they would dig, just past the little campus grave-yard. The slip of paper for the fear would be tied to a balloon to be set free and float away over the mansion.

Micah waited outside the chapel, until Snoop wandered outside, trailing a balloon behind him, clutched in his fingers.

"Snoop," Micah said.

Snoop lifted his other hand to block out the sun. "Hey, white boy."

"We need to talk."

"I'm kinda in the middle of something."

Micah reached out to grip Snoop's arm but pulled back at the last second. Instead, Micah narrowed his eyes at the man. "It's important."

Snoop raised an eyebrow, but relented. He let go of his balloon and followed Micah around the chapel, past the cafeteria, to the back, where they used to crush cans together.

"What is it?" Snoop said.

"One week ago, a dark-skinned man came onto campus, with a knife."

Snoop shrugged, but Micah could see the hesitation written on his face. He had no comment.

"I think that man was here to kill you," Micah said.

"You got no proof of that."

"Cut the shit, Snoop. I saw you meeting with someone out in the woods yesterday. Who was that?"

Snoop bit his lip and said nothing.

"Want to know what I think?" Micah said. "I think you do have the smallpox, and the cartel is trying to get it back from you. I think you double-crossed them, and you've been on the run from Dos Cruces for the last few years."

Snoop crossed his arms and sucked on his teeth. "Hmm. That's an interesting way to look at it."

"And the other day, in the laundry room, you were going to tell me all about it. Your conscience was weighing on you. You wanted to get honest with me, but you couldn't do it."

Snoop's crossed arms slipped as his face fell. "You don't know anything, white boy."

"Then educate me."

"Why should I? Why should I tell you anything?"

"Because you have to tell someone, Snoop. You know what they say about secrets. You know how being dishonest is going to catch up with you. If you're sincere about starting a new life, you can't keep lying. You know it's going to lead you back to a drink."

"Fine. That's not Dos Cruces after me."

"How do you know?"

"Because I never left Dos Cruces. I don't know how you got away from the Sinaloa, but Dos Cruces is not like that. Once you're Cruces, it's for your whole life."

"So who is after you?"

"The Serbians, dummy. They want their property back. That was probably who you saw in the woods the other day, with the knife. They must have finally figured out I stole their shit. I'm sure they know where I am now, and they're coming for it."

"So you do have it."

Snoop took a step back and bumped into the side of the brick building. Held out his hand for support. "I've been running from these people for years. Always looking over my shoulder, waiting for some rando on the street to put a bullet in me. I just want this shit to be over with."

"What does that mean? What were you going to ask me, in the laundry room the other day?"

"This is bigger than me. There are things I can't tell you about. Not now, not ever. But I need help, Micah. I don't want to do this anymore. I don't want to be this person, always sprinting away from danger."

"What? What don't you want to do? What's going to happen, Snoop?"

"I don't have the smallpox. That part was true. Dos Cruces has it, and it's somewhere nearby. What I do have is the code to open the lockbox it's in. That's been my security blanket this whole time. If I didn't have that, my people would have probably killed me long ago. They can't open the box without it. So when it's time, they tell me where it is and who I'm supposed to sell it to. Then I put in the code, hand off the lockbox, and I'm done. I'm on a plane to Vietnam, and I never have to see them ever again. Or, maybe the Serbians find a way to catch me and kill me before I can leave."

"Why do this at all? I don't understand why you can't walk away from it."

"That's the part I can't tell you."

"Fine. So, you're waiting for a signal?"

Snoop nodded. "And it's going to be soon, because I'm out, the day after tomorrow. If they don't contact me before then, this whole thing collapses and it's not my problem anymore."

"And you don't know who the buyer is."

Snoop shook his head. "Told them to use someone I didn't know. Someone not involved in the whole thing, so when I punch the code in the box, Dos Cruces won't be directly involved. They're supposed to be far away. That was part of the arrangement."

Micah immediately thought of Nash as the buyer. He fit all the right criteria. "You trust your people to stay away?"

Tears formed at the corners of his eyes. "I don't. I think they're going to kill me, no matter what I do. They let me come here to treatment because I told them I had to do this. But Dos Cruces isn't like it used to be. Not about *familia* anymore. They won't let me walk away, knowing what I know. You've been in the life before, Micah. You know how these people are."

Snoop wiped his wet eyes on his sleeve. "Help me."

Micah felt his heart tugged in so many directions at once. He certainly knew the pain of having to do things for terrible people when you didn't want to. And he believed Snoop wanted to escape and not have to go through with this horrible transaction.

But Snoop had lied before.

PART III

YOU'RE ONLY AS SICK AS YOUR SECRETS

DAY 27.1

MICAH AWOKE WITH a sense of urgency. Today was Nash's last day, as was Leighton's. Snoop had one more day until his graduation. Micah was also facing only one more sleep until his final day. But none of those timelines mattered if this smallpox sale went through as planned.

Micah understood that Snoop felt he had no choice. He knew his future actions were terrible, but it would be the last terrible thing he would have to do before he could be free.

And Micah knew that the cartel would never let Snoop be free. Micah had tried to convince Snoop of this yesterday, to give himself up to the feds and tell them everything. Snoop had spent years making the police and FBI believe he'd left Dos Cruces and had no involvement with the smallpox.

But he could fix all that with one conversation.

Snoop seemed to believe he had a chance. That, with Micah's help, he could make the deal and escape with his life, plus with twenty-eight days of sobriety under his belt.

The plan was this: Snoop would go through with the sale tomorrow, and then tip Micah off. Micah would contact Frank and Gavin, and then they would follow the buyer and intercept the smallpox. At least, that's what Micah and Snoop had discussed. But Micah didn't know if he could let this man walk away without consequences. And if doing so would ruin Micah's chance to help his brother.

Whatever his reasons, Snoop was about to commit a terrible crime.

Across the room, Nash sat up in bed, yawning loudly. Nash hadn't spoken to Micah in several days. His roommate glared at him anytime their paths crossed. Maybe Nash thought Micah had tipped off Dryden and Oscar, to persuade them to search the room. But if Nash did have any contraband, he'd moved it out before then. So what was he worried about?

Nash threw on some clothes, occasionally glancing over at Micah, but never going so far as to actually speak. This quiet tension between them had to break at some point, but Micah was unwilling to offer an olive branch. Nash only served to stand in the way now.

The odds were good that tomorrow, when the deal went down, Nash would be the one to receive the smallpox. And Micah would follow him and take him down.

Micah would end this.

When his roommate left, Micah got out of bed and dressed quickly.

As soon as he'd descended the stairs and ventured into the hallway, he noticed a significant increase in the population. People hanging around, talking on the payphones, walking up the hallway toward the mansion. In the little library, he found a dozen more chatting, hugging, talking on *cellphones.*

Reunion day. That monthly shindig at The Stone when former patients surfaced to hang out, attend lectures, and catch up with counselors and old class- mates. The ones who'd been sober a full year would return to claim their mugs during the announcements.

Many of the visitors were smiling, chatting excitedly. They dished out hugs and kisses to their loved ones, commenting about how fresh and vibrant they looked after a few weeks of sobriety. Some were still hesitant, which was understandable. A few weeks off booze wasn't enough to undo years of lies and betrayal.

Micah weaved through the visitors on his way to the basement, nodding politely at anyone who made eye contact with him.

Micah went to morning announcements as usual, where he watched five former patients who were now sober for a year get up and collect the mugs they'd painted during their time here.

After the extended announcements session, Micah decided to skip the morning lecture about the family disease of alcoholism, because he'd sat through that one a couple times already.

He strolled around campus, breathing in the crisp January air and trying to puzzle out how this was all going to come together. The crowded rooms and halls of reunion day made finding a quiet space challenging. He wanted to be alone with his thoughts.

First, he ascended to the third floor, the one that led to the attic. He wasn't technically supposed to be here, but since he was a short-timer, the staff tended to leave him alone. After all, he was patient of the week this week, an honor that came with zero privileges. Except that maybe the nurses might turn a blind eye if Micah wanted to explore the nooks and crannies of the building.

He opened the attic door and climbed the short spiral staircase. Found himself in a dusty and dimly-lit room with dense rows of shelves, only a foot or two of walking space between them. Each o those shelves housed hundreds upon hundreds of mugs. They were painted every color of the rainbow, many of them also with dates etched into the paint. The sobriety dates of the patients who'd made them.

Micah strolled through the tight space between the shelves, examining some of these dates. Many of them were older than a year ago. These former patients should have returned already to claim their mugs, but they were likely drinking or getting high. Rutting in their addiction.

Micah changed his mind. This was not a good place to get into the right headspace to solve problems. He skipped down the stairs and walked out the front door, thinking he'd just meander around the campus. Do a lap to the cafeteria and back. Except, when he circled the kitchen to return back toward the mansion, he found something unexpected in the can-smashing area. Nash and Leighton, huddled together with a third person. A newer patient at treatment, someone who'd only been here a week or so. Micah couldn't remember the guy's name.

And they weren't only huddling together. A transaction was happening. Nash passed a brown paper bag to the guy, who opened it, sniffed, and then removed a clump of bills from his pocket. The guy passed the cash to Leighton, who thumbed through it and then shoved the money into her purse. Nash and the guy shook hands, then the guy's eyes widened when he looked in Micah's direction. He flicked his head at Micah.

Nash and Leighton both gasped when they saw him.

"What the hell?" Nash said. His lips curled into a snarl. "Micah? You've got to be shitting me."

"You nosy prick," Leighton said.

Nash drew a knife from his back pocket. "I know you went through my stuff, you piece of shit."

Standing fifty feet away, Micah now knew that Nash definitely had written that strange and cryptic liability note for Micah's Hot Seat. But the reference wasn't about the smallpox at all. It was about selling drugs.

Nash broke out into a run at Micah. Knife raised. Shouting.

Micah was unarmed, and not in any shape to fight. His senses came alive, and he prepared himself to flee back to the mansion.

From around the chapel emerged Nurse Oscar and two uniformed cops, also running toward Nash. Micah recognized them as Zell and Gillespie, the two cops who'd questioned him the day after the stabbing.

Oscar was pointing and yelling at the knife-wielding man rushing at Micah. The cops sprinted.

Nash would get there first.

Micah lowered his center of gravity a few inches and prepared to meet Nash head-on. A taser dart flew through the air, whizzing past Nash. The cop had missed.

Then, a half-second before Nash arrived, Micah sunk to his knees. Leaned to the side. Jabbed a closed fist at Nash's bad knee.

Nash tripped and barreled forward into the ground. The knife tumbled into the grass next to him. Before Micah could dart after it, Nash had recovered the blade. He spun onto his back and raised the knife, jabbing it forward.

Micah kicked it out of his hand. The knife sailed through the air and landed harmlessly, ten feet away.

Nash put his hands on the ground to push himself to his feet, but a revolver hammer cocked behind them.

"Don't move," Officer Zell said, now hovering above Nash. Pistol out and pointed at the man's head.

Zell snatched Nash by the shoulder and hauled him up, then wrenched his hands back to restrain him. Nash roared as the cop slapped the cuffs on him.

Nash stared Micah down. "Who the fuck *are* you, man?"

"I'm Micah."

Zell dragged Nash away, and Micah turned to see Gillespie with his gun pointed at Leighton and the third person as the cop motioned for them to drop to their knees.

Oscar, panting, stopped in front of Micah. "You okay?"

"I'm fine."

"Sorry about all the drama," Oscar said. "We didn't know you would be out here this morning."

"It's okay. I'm just… just a little confused."

Oscar tilted his head at Nash, who was now being pushed toward an unmarked cop car in the parking lot. "He's been here three times, and we've always suspected him of moving drugs. Wasn't until this morning we overheard him making plans to come out here with his partner Leighton to make a deal."

Micah looked back at Leighton as Gillespie was digging through her purse, pulling out needles and baggies full of pills. She cackled at Micah, then made a playful stabbing motion at his stomach.

Micah had to wonder why Gavin hadn't shut this

down to prevent the cops from coming onto campus, as he had with the scissors incident. He must not have even known it was happening.

Who was in charge here? Who determined what was allowed on campus? Made no sense.

"Crazy," Micah said to Oscar. "I'm glad you caught them."

Oscar winced and ran a hand through his hair to slick it back. "We would appreciate it if you didn't spread this out through the patients. We like to keep these matters quiet, if possible."

"Sure, I understand."

Oscar grimaced as he looked over Micah's shoulder. "Oh, crap."

Micah spun to see Executive Director Rhonda Delaney stomping through the parking lot, toward the cops. Her eyes wide with fury, her jacket flailing behind her as she power-walked.

"What the hell is going on here?" she shouted at the officers. "You are not allowed here."

Oscar stepped in front of her and spread his hands out, preventing her from advancing. "They're not allowed in the building, Rhonda. They're within their rights to be here in the parking lot."

"What?" she said. "You knew about this?"

"I did," Oscar said. "I called them to come arrest Nash and Leighton."

Rhonda gritted her teeth. "Damn you, Oscar. How

dare you do this. Do you know what this means if it gets out? What this could do to Cornerstone's reputation?"

"I do. I know exactly what it means. And I decided anyway that calling the police was what needed to happen. Fire me if you want, but it's done now."

She dragged clawed hands down her face, leaving white marks on her skin. At first, Micah had been puzzled why she was so angry. But then, as this perfectly professional-looking woman threw her tantrum, Micah understood. Dryden hadn't been the one to cover up Micah's stabbing. This Rhonda woman had been behind the whole thing. Protecting The Stone's reputation at all costs.

"In my office. Fifteen minutes," Rhonda said, then she spun on her heels and stormed back toward the mansion.

"Holy shit," Micah said, once Rhonda had left them.

"Yeah," Oscar said. "I really did enjoy working here."

"Sorry, Oscar."

Oscar patted Micah on the shoulder. "That's okay. Sometimes it's worth it, to do the right thing. I hope you'll remember that for later on when you need it."

Micah nodded as Oscar walked back toward the mansion. Micah then leaned against a car in the lot as the two cops ushered Nash and Leighton into the backs of their cars.

This whole place was swimming in a lake of crazy-juice.

Micah started back toward the mansion when Snoop

came sprinting across the parking lot, waving his arms at Micah. Frantically rushing to meet him.

"What is it?" Micah said after he'd met Snoop halfway.

"Now," Snoop said. "It's happening now. Not tomorrow. In one hour, at the edge of the property. In the bushes, just past the front entrance. One hour."

Snoop turned and ran, and Micah realized he needed to get to a phone right away. But, then he watched the cop cars driving away, with Nash in one and Leighton in the other. If neither one of them was the buyer, who was?

DAY 27.2

HENRIETTA DRYDEN STARED at the address on a slip of paper. Pine Ridge office building, Southwest 89th Street, in Oklahoma City. She'd never been there before. The building was supposedly abandoned, but that's where she'd been ordered to take the delivery she would receive today.

She didn't know who she was meeting, and she didn't know why. She also didn't know the contents of the package. Something bad, no doubt. But, she knew what completing this transaction would do for her.

This task would keep her past in the past.

The public had been told she'd resigned over an affair with a staffer, but that had been the lie to cover up the real evil. The money she'd embezzled from her own mayoral campaign. The fundraiser money that had been pledged to charity.

How many times would she have to pay for that sin?

At least one more, apparently. She was supposed to forage into the woods and dig up a lockbox, stored at exact GPS coordinates. Then she would meet someone on campus, and that person would have a keycode for her. She would drive to Oklahoma City, deliver the lockbox and the keycode, and then she would be done. At that office building, they would show her the proof of her campaign embezzling, and she would take possession of it. She would have the only copy of the documents that proved what a misguided person she'd been.

She could destroy them. Eradicate them.

She could have her life back if these Dos Cruces people didn't betray her. But, there was no reason to assume they *would* keep their word. What choice did she have, though? She'd already lost her political career and her marriage over one stupid sin. Now, there was a chance to keep her freedom. She had to take it.

In the bathroom, Dryden opened the medicine cabinet and removed her toothbrush and toothpaste. She ran the water and brushed her teeth, enjoying the feeling of scrubbing away the impurities on those perfect, white surfaces. Being fresh and clean.

She took one last look at her office, with the little blocks of all six primary feelings sitting on the end table. Being a counselor here for these last few years had been a memorable experience. Even with little shits like Micah, who lied and manipulated and always seemed to find a way to win. Even with people like him, she still liked this job.

Maybe she would be able to continue to do this job.

She closed up the files on her desk, shut down her laptop, and left her office, for what she hoped wasn't the last time. If this all went well, no one here would ever have to know.

Dryden silently glided down the hall toward Rhonda's office at the far end of the second floor. Along the way, she nodded at two patients and five other people who were reunion day attendees, presumably.

She stopped outside the director's office and extended an arm to knock, but the door swung open. There stood nurse Oscar, a tear streaking down his cheek.

"What?" she said.

Oscar sighed. "Goodbye, Henrietta. It's been nice working with you. I know we didn't often agree, but I respected your integrity, at least."

With that, he planted a foot and strode past her, leaving Dryden alone to stare into Rhonda's office.

Rhonda reclined in a chair behind her enormous desk, her hands folded in front of her. "Yes, Henrietta? Did you need something?"

Dryden stepped inside, her thumb pointed behind her. "What was that about?"

Rhonda cleared her throat. "Nurse Oscar is no longer employed at Cornerstone, and it's not something I'm willing to discuss in detail. Is there something I can do for you?"

"The scissors."

"Not you too," Rhonda said, rolling her eyes.

"Where are they?"

Rhonda sighed, then she opened one of her desk drawers and pulled out a Ziploc baggie. Dropped it on the desk. Inside were a pair of orange-handled scissors, coated in blood.

"Are you happy now?" she said.

"This isn't right."

"You're one to talk about what is and isn't right. Your time as mayor of Guthrie? I know all about it. Having an affair with your staffer? Really, Henrietta. I hope he was worth it, to throw away your career and your marriage."

"That's not what happened."

Rhonda cocked her head. "It's not? Do tell."

"This isn't about me. This is about you covering up serious crimes in the name of The Stone's reputation. Allowing drug dealers to get away with it. Quietly kicking out pedophiles instead of sending them to prison. Allowing patients to stab other patients."

"Are you done? Because you know what? I don't care who my counselors are, or who my nurses are. You can all be replaced. I hired you cheap because I knew you were broken, and I have a stack of résumés of people who want to work here."

Dryden gritted her teeth and said nothing.

"You are free to resign at any time," Rhonda said. "And after you leave, Cornerstone will remain."

A sudden flash of awareness came over Dryden. That small physical tilt, like a tiny shot of adrenaline, when her body shifted to accompany a change of opinion. A realization. The shiver began in her toes and worked its way up through her spine, dissipating in her shoulders.

Five minutes ago, Dryden had wished to keep her job after what she was about to do today. Now, she realized, she never wanted to see this place again. When this transaction was done, maybe all she had to do was call in an anonymous tip about it, making sure that The Stone's name came up as the place the deal had originated.

"Cornerstone will always remain?" Dryden said. "Is that what you think?"

Rhonda nodded.

"You might be surprised, Rhonda, at what's about to happen today. This might not be the sort of thing you can sweep under the rug."

Rhonda stood up. "What are you talking about?"

Dryden crossed the room and snatched the scissors from the desk. Rhonda tried to grab them out of her hands, but Dryden pulled back, out of reach. Next, she yanked Rhonda's cellphone from her desk, shoved it in her pocket, and snapped her landline phone free, breaking the cord.

Dryden reversed course and rushed out of the room, then slammed the door shut. Yanked the scissors out of the baggie, and then jammed the point of the scissors into the crack between the door and door frame, imprisoning Rhonda inside her office.

As Rhonda yelled from the other side, Dryden stepped back, looking at what she'd done. This was final. There was no coming back from this.

DAY 27.3

PAST THE PARKING lot, the front end of the Cornerstone campus led out to a simple dirt road that connected to a gravel road, and that connected to a paved road in town. Two tall columns marked the entrance, with a small stone fence that bordered the front of the property. Five-foot hedges lined the outer side of the fence, and that's where Micah and Frank waited in hiding. Nestled in the abyss between the hedges and the fence.

Micah's heart pounded. Had trouble swallowing. Everything felt so razor-thin and flimsy.

He had not told Frank the full extent of the plan. Micah didn't exactly know what would happen when this deal went down, but he didn't know if he could allow Snoop to walk away from it cleanly. For whatever reason, Snoop was selling this biological weapon to someone, and Micah shouldn't let that happen. His stomach rumbled with guilt about the decision. He wanted Snoop to get sober. He wanted Snoop to have the internal freedom that came with a life rid of the slavery of addiction.

But Snoop might have to do that from inside a prison cell.

He hadn't shared any of this with Frank, had instead kept it inside, trying to play cool. Frank had given him a few cross-eyed looks, but Micah kept his mouth shut. How could he explain to Frank that a part of him wanted to allow this man to get away with it?

The atmosphere hung thick around Micah's head. He pushed air in and out of his lungs with too much exertion. Something was not right with this setup. He could feel it.

"Where's Gavin?" Micah said.

"He's not coming. He's going to stay back at the office building in case we don't intercept them here."

"What about his SWAT team?"

Frank shrugged. "I honestly don't know. Gavin is managing all that, and he didn't give me any details. I assume they're with him."

"What time is it?"

Frank lifted a wrist to check his gold watch, a retirement present from the Denver Police Department. "10:30."

"Shit. It's been over an hour."

"You think Snoop's people are late?"

Micah considered it. The frantic look on Snoop's

usually-calm face when he'd sprinted through the parking lot to inform Micah about the new timeline. The way his hands had been shaking.

This whole situation was wrong.

"No," Micah said. "I think he lied to me to remove us from the equation."

Micah scooted out from behind the hedge, fighting his way through the scratchy brambles. Frank held his hands in front of his face to protect himself as he pushed through after Micah.

"What do we do now?" Frank said. "Any idea where to go?"

"Follow me," Micah said as he jogged through the parking lot. The pain in his side was now a blip. He felt almost normal.

He and Frank approached the Cornerstone mansion, navigated through the crowds of smokers, chatters, people meandering here and there. Quite a few of them looked askance at the two men dodging between all the bodies. Micah didn't care. If the deal had already happened, they were in big trouble.

Past the mansion, they skirted across the basketball courts and into the rolling hills of the woods beyond. Some late morning frost still clung to the grass under-foot, and Micah's feet crunched through it as he jogged as quickly as his partially-healed body would allow.

Then he saw it.

Snoop, standing under the shade of a massive pecan tree a football field away. Twenty feet to Snoop's left,

Henrietta Dryden, carrying a dark rectangle the size of a carry-on suitcase. The lockbox. Micah could see the bits of dirt clinging to the side from here.

Dryden was the buyer.

She had dug up the cache with the smallpox from the woods behind campus, and now Snoop would give her the code to open it and remove the deadly poison.

They were opposite each other, like two duelers ready to draw pistols. Something about the looks on each of their faces struck Micah as terribly lonely. Terribly lost. Their eyes locked, each making a slow and deliberate march toward the other, as if caught in tractor beams.

Except they weren't the only people out here in the woods behind campus. Something entered Micah's vision from the left. Creeping up behind Henrietta were four men in dark clothing, each of them carrying large guns.

Frank pointed. "Serbians."

DAY 27.4

MICAH ACCEPTED THE Beretta 9mm from Frank, and they both pointed their weapons at the group of men advancing toward Snoop and Dryden. They were too far away from the action to shoot, but that didn't matter. Soon enough, one of two things was going to happen: either Snoop and Dryden would make this deal, or the Serbians would kill both of them. If the Serbians were smart, they would wait until after Snoop had given her the code to open the case. They probably knew that.

Snoop and Dryden met in the middle of the field, each of them oblivious to the creeping Serbians. Also, both seemingly surprised to encounter the other person. Dos Cruces had been smart in the way they'd set this all up. Keep both of them blind so they couldn't give each other away.

Dense trees to the left. Dense trees to the right. The field in which Dryden and Snoop stood was about fifty feet by fifty feet, a clearing with fewer trees, slightly angled at the crest of a hill.

And as Dryden held out the lockbox, presumably so Snoop could type in the code to unlock it, Micah and Frank broke into a run. And not only because of the threat of the Serbians on the left. If Micah could stop Snoop from entering that code, the lockbox would stay shut.

Micah was about to shout at Dryden to drop the box when he noticed three more figures on the right, hiding behind a tree on Snoop's side. Three dark-skinned men. Had to be Dos Cruces, here to make sure the deal would happen, fend off the Serbians, and then probably kill Snoop once he'd opened the box.

As Micah narrowed the distance, Snoop turned, and his eyes opened wide. His mouth dropped open. "No!" he shouted. "Micah, get back!"

Dryden also noticed Micah and Frank barreling toward them, and she dropped the lockbox and spun on her heels to flee. One of the Serbians emerged from behind a tree and snatched her by the wrist. He twisted her around and pulled her to him as a human shield. Laced one arm below her neck and pointed a Zastava PAP M85 machine pistol over her shoulder, aimed at the cartel members fifty feet away.

Snoop hit the ground, his hands over his head.

Dryden screamed and thrashed about, but the Serbian was too strong. She raised her knee and slammed a heel down onto the top of his boot, which got his attention. His grip around her neck relaxed, and she was about to break free when a shot blasted from the Dos Cruces side of the clearing. Her head snapped back. Her arms flailed a moment longer and then she fell face-first into the grass.

Across the field, a cartel member had stepped out from behind the tree to shoot her. He'd probably been aiming for the Serbian. Now exposed, the Serbian's body twisted from a hail of bullets, and he sunk to the ground, his body flattening on top of Dryden's. The other Serbians held cover behind three different trees.

Micah lifted the 9mm and popped off a few shots. He hit his target in the chest, and the man fell to one knee, then he popped right back up. Had to be a Kevlar vest.

One of the Serbians was wielding an AK-47, and he leaned out from cover and mowed down two of the three cartel members with a single sweep of his weapon. The other Dos Cruces member dropped and rolled, then braced himself against a thick tree stump. Popped up to squeeze off a shot and caught one of the Serbians in the shoulder.

Micah and Frank were closing the distance. Hopelessly outgunned, but still running hard and fast.

Micah aimed low and shot a Serbian in the leg, which knocked the man off balance.

Twenty feet ahead, a rotted log blocked Micah's path. The log wasn't much, but it would provide eighteen inches of cover. He dimly recalled sitting on that same log on one of his exploration trips out here.

This whole time, the smallpox had been buried not far away.

"There," Micah shouted. Frank didn't need any coaching, and he dropped into a roll once they were close. Micah flattened himself and crawled the last few feet to nestle behind the log. It hid them from the Serbians, but they were partially exposed to the Dos Cruces guy. But the cartel member had enough to worry about, with the Serbians lobbying a steady stream of bullets at him.

At one end of the clearing, the two remaining Serbians hid behind a tree. On the other end of the clearing, the cartel member hid behind the stump. Frank and Micah were both panting, staying low behind their cover. Micah reached out a hand and touched the soggy wood of the rotting log. It wouldn't hold up to many bullets.

Snoop was prone, his hands still above his head. The lockbox sat in the grass, five feet away.

Everyone had their eyes on the lockbox.

Frank lifted his head a fraction of an inch, but Micah jerked him back down. "Frank, don't. They have vests and automatic weapons."

"What are we supposed to do? Sit here and wait for them to shoot us?"

"I don't know. Let me think."

The cartel member shouted something in Spanish as he reloaded. The two Serbians replied in a language Micah didn't recognize.

Nothing but the sound of the woods arose for a few seconds. Snoop raised his head and observed the standoff around him. He craned his neck back and forth, looking toward Micah, then at the Serbians. Then at the open woods to his right.

Snoop pushed himself onto his elbow, while still keeping his head down. He looked directly at Micah. Their eyes met.

Micah shook his head. *Don't you even think about it, you stupid son of a bitch.*

But, Snoop had apparently not read Micah's mind. In a flash, Snoop jumped to his feet and sprinted off into the woods. The Serbians shot at him, but only a couple times. Snoop zig-zagged as he ran, and in a few more seconds, he'd disappeared over a hill. Gone.

Neither the Serbians nor the cartel would leave their hiding spots to chase after him, exposing themselves to gunfire from the other side. The lockbox was here, on the ground. Maybe, at the moment, nobody realized that Snoop was still the only person with the code to open it.

"What do you think happens now?" Frank said.

"Hopefully, they kill each other," Micah said.

One of the Serbians turned his head toward the log, and he raised his AK. Spit some shots, and Micah and

Frank flattened themselves to the ground. The log rumbled as shots peppered it. Micah had to hope this piece of wet lumber wouldn't collapse under the strain of the bullets. Wouldn't last long.

The Serbians paused, and then started shouting at each other. The air changed. A light breeze picked up. Micah listened to the sound of a magazine clicking into place, coming from behind the tree stump.

The cartel member bellowed something in Spanish.

The Serbians shouted back at him.

Without warning, both Serbians took bullets in the head. Fast. Clinical. Micah turned to see three men with SWAT written across their chests, in full-body armor and helmets, hustling through the woods, AR-15 rifles raised.

The cartel member popped up from behind the stump, screaming as he pulled the trigger. A SWAT member cut him down where he stood. Bullets punctured his groin, chest, and forehead in three indistinguishable blasts. He fell to his knees, then flat onto his face.

The agents rushed past the log. One of them pointed his rifle at the dead cartel member. One approached the Serbians and Dryden's body. The final SWAT team member spun around and raised his rifle at Micah and Frank.

And they both dropped their guns and placed their hands on top of their heads.

"Mr. Mueller, Mr. Reed," the agent said. "Are you hurt?"

Micah stood, a little dazed from the ferocity of all the gunfire. Frank, however, jumped to his feet, scrambled over the log, and then snatched up the lockbox.

GAVIN HAD WATCHED the men in the white trucks unloading storage containers all morning. As he and Agent Hessler sat at the edge of the Pine Ridge office building parking lot in their car with its deeply tinted windows, they witnessed the whole operation take place. Nondescript storage bins unloaded from the truck, carried into the propped-open back door. No one stopped to open the containers or check them. That would happen indoors.

Gavin only noted one soldier and three others. The others weren't large or armed. They were middle-aged, potbellied, and seemingly not trained in any military way. While the soldier kept an eye out, these other three wouldn't have noticed any intrusions at all.

After the last of the truck had been unloaded and all the scientist-types went inside, Gavin relaxed. The armed guard, however, started patrolling the building.

He walked a loop around it, disappearing behind the south and reappearing around the north side. Two-minute rotations, quick pace.

"Marshal?" Agent Hessler said.

"Yes, Agent Hessler?"

"How long are we going to wait?"

Gavin checked his watch. "I was hoping Frank or Micah would call by now. But, maybe things are taking longer than they expected."

And if all were going according to plan, Frank and Frank alone would be in possession of that smallpox now. If Gavin's suspicions turned out to be true.

Hessler reached in the back seat and opened a bag, and then withdrew his M4 carbine rifle. "I'd just like to remind you, sir, that I have a six o'clock flight."

"Right," Gavin said. "Let's do this."

Gavin and Hessler exited the rental car and crossed the parking lot after the guard disappeared one more time around the southern side of the building. Gavin hurried to the northern edge where this guard would be making his appearance in approximately one minute, if he kept his same schedule. Hessler nestled at the corner, with Gavin right behind him.

Exactly one minute later, the guard emerged, his meaty arms preceding his body. Hessler snatched the exposed arm and spun it, then pushed the guard against the building, smashing his face into the concrete. Flesh scraped as the guard grunted.

Gavin handcuffed the man and looped a zip tie

around his feet while he struggled in vain to break free. Hessler lowered the guard to the ground.

"You have any idea who you're messing with?" the guard said, snarling.

Gavin took a length of duct tape from the roll in his hand and slapped it over the guard's mouth. "No, but I'm about to find out." He used one last length of cable to secure the guard's feet to a bicycle rack attached to the side of the building.

With the guard out of the way, Gavin and Hessler rounded the building to enter from the back. It was the same quiet first floor, but now the lights were on. He removed his pistol and squinted, checking for motion on the first floor. He didn't expect to find any, and after a few seconds of stillness, he lock-picked the door.

Gavin and his temporary partner climbed the stairs, weapons raised. Gavin breathed through his nose and out his mouth, trying to settle his pulse to a reasonable level. Chest thumping. He didn't anticipate any more resistance, but no reason to be careless.

They crested the stairs and padded silently out into the main room. The secret door from before was wide open, light on. Gavin pointed at the door and motioned for Hessler to follow him. As Gavin peeked past the open door, he found a brightly-lit room on the other side.

Raised his weapon, but the room was empty.

Inside were the same server racks and counters from before, but now, the counters were filled with beakers, test tube racks, and sealed containers. Non-slip mats covering the floor. And hanging from one of the server racks were three yellow full-body HazMat suits.

A staging area to receive the smallpox and prepare it.

As much as this scene horrified Gavin—because he knew exactly what all these items were for—a little piece of him finally felt vindicated.

"What is all this?" Hessler whispered.

"Mobile lab for biological weapons," Gavin said.

In the distance, the bark of a laugh carried from across the office. Hessler and Gavin both spun. Gavin turned his ear toward the sound, waiting for more. He could hear the slightest warble of conversation coming from somewhere on this floor.

He raised his gun and left the server room, with Hessler following behind. Gavin pivoted and entered the hallway to the right, into an open room filled with cubicles. The voices grew louder, coming from the end of the room.

This room had the same layout as downstairs: cube farm in the middle, with offices lining the edges of the room. Except one wall was absent, and that's where the voices emanated from. Gavin ducked down into the cubicles and crept toward the edge, then leaned out. The open space at one end emptied into a kitchen. Standing around a box of pizza on a red table were three men in lab coats, each of them munching on slices.

Gavin pointed for Hessler to sneak to the other end of the cubicle row, and Hessler didn't need any further

275

instructions. He and Gavin approached the kitchen from opposite sides of the cube farm.

When he reached the end, Gavin popped up, gun raised.

All three men dropped their slices of pizza back into the box.

"Who the hell are you?" said one of the men as he wiped his greasy hands on his lab coat.

Gavin drew back his pistol's slide. "You have three seconds to tell me who's in charge, or I start shooting."

"Me," said one of the men. He was short and pudgy, with a large bald spot in the middle of his curly hair.

"Hessler," Gavin said.

Hessler appeared in the kitchen from the left side. "Yessir."

"Please detain these other two and take them outside."

"You really want me to wait outside?"

Gavin frowned. "Yes, I do."

Hessler used zip ties to bind the hands of the two other men, and they put up no fight at all. They stared at the remaining man as Hessler carried them out, and the pudgy man mouthed *say nothing* to them.

Once Gavin and the remaining man were alone, Baldy put his hands into the pockets of his lab coat. Smug look on his face.

"You have no idea who you're messing with," he said.

"Funny. That's what your guard outside said before I shut him up with duct tape. Who do you work for? Russians? China?"

The man shook his head. "I'm not telling you a thing."

"I've seen your mobile lab back there. There's no point in lying to me. My name is Gavin Belmont, and I'm a US Marshal."

"Get stuffed, Marshal."

Gavin lowered his pistol and shot at the floor, near the man's feet.

"Jesus Christ," he screamed as he jumped out of the way.

Gavin raised his weapon. "Don't move. Why did you set up here and then clear it all out?"

The man gulped, tried to catch his breath. "We saw you sniffing around and didn't want you to find anything."

"Why not move locations? Why come back here to set up shop again?"

"Because," the man said, leaning against the table for support, "we had no way to get word to the courier about a location change. We thought you were off the scent."

"Who do you work for?"

The man shook his head. He wheezed and swayed, then put two fingers of one hand on the wrist of his other hand, checking his pulse.

"Please hold your arms out, like this," Gavin said, taking one of his hands off his gun to demonstrate holding his arm parallel to the floor.

The man raised an eyebrow but did as he was told.

Gavin pivoted and shot the man in the hand. He wailed and fell to the floor, thrashing, sending droplets of blood into the air, landing on the table and on slices of pizza.

"Who do you work for?"

The man grimaced. "I think I'm having a heart attack."

"Who do you work for? I'm not going to ask you again," Gavin said, pointing his pistol at the man's head.

"Vanton Industries, okay?"

Gavin lowered the gun. "Vanton? What the hell is that?"

"It's a biotech company. And no, you've never heard of it before, you idiot."

Gavin gritted his teeth. "Be a smartass all you want, because you're going to prison for the rest of your life. I'm a fed, and you're trafficking in biological weapons, dumbass."

The man clutched his bleeding hand. "We won't see a day in prison."

"Why not?"

The man said nothing.

Gavin raised the pistol and closed one eye to aim down the site. "Hold up your other hand."

"Okay, okay," the man shouted as he put his hands over his head. Blood dribbled down his temple. "We're here on behalf of the NSA."

"The what?"

"The National fucking Security Administration, alright?"

Gavin's world collapsed to a pinhole. The NSA?

Gavin's own government had been trying to acquire this N5A9 strain?

"Why would the NSA want smallpox?"

"Would it be better if the Serbians had it? Or that cluster of disorganized Mexican gangs that call themselves Dos Cruces? Maybe if—"

"Stop talking. If you're lying to me, I'm going to shoot you somewhere a lot more painful than your hand."

The man on the floor swayed, then slumped, holding his hand against his chest. His shirt had turned into a red mess. His breathing slowed, returning to normal. "I'm not lying. I swear it."

Footsteps thundered into the room behind Gavin.

"Everything's okay, Agent Hessler," Gavin said, without turning around.

"What happened here?" Hessler said.

Gavin holstered his weapon. "This is what the truth looks like."

MICAH DRIFTED OFF to sleep, but only for a moment. The overhead speaker at Oklahoma City's Will Rogers Airport squawked and ripped him back to consciousness. These chairs near the check-in were so terribly uncomfortable. He shuffled his feet along the floor underneath, the surface recently buffed to a slick shine.

As he became fully awake, he experienced a moment of panic that he might have missed his target. How long had he been napping? Five minutes? Fifty?

He lifted his phone to check the time. Maybe fifteen minutes since he'd last looked. Micah considered walking around to hunt, but this current spot was the best place to eye the oncoming traffic headed for the security line.

But, Micah didn't have to continue his internal debate much longer. Because the next person to come through the revolving door from the parking garage was Snoop Jiménez, with a suitcase under each arm.

Snoop stopped dead in his tracks as Micah rose to his feet.

"Hey, Snoop," Micah said among the din.

Snoop shook his head, clenched his suitcases close, and pivoted left to walk past Micah.

Micah closed the distance between them and held up his phone, with 911 entered on the keypad. "Wait. I just want to ask you a few questions. I don't have to call the cops if you sit down and talk with me. You've still got plenty of time to make your flight."

Snoop mused on this for a second, and then his eyes drifted to the security line, where three police officers were standing with some TSA employees, chatting.

Snoop relented, shoulders falling. He moped over to the uncomfortable chairs where Micah had been sitting, then he slumped into one. The chairs were like a long, connected set of mini-benches, facing the front entrance of the airport.

As soon as Micah had sat, he noticed the weariness on Snoop's face. The bags under his eyes. The puffiness that suggested he'd been crying. His clothes were wrinkled and his hair was uncombed.

"How did you find me?" Snoop said. His voice cracked as he spoke. He kept his face forward, not turning his body to engage with Micah.

"I figured the ticket for the plane from Tulsa had to be

a decoy, and there is only one flight to Vietnam today out of this airport. Wasn't hard."

"You're like one of those fishes that attaches itself to a shark, catching a free ride to wherever. What do you want?"

"I want to know why."

Snoop pivoted in his chair. His eyes flashed, his lips curled into a snarl. "Why *what*?"

"Why did you tell me you were meeting the buyer at the hedges by the front, when you were actually meeting her back in the woods?"

Snoop turned back to face the entrance of the airport, his wet eyes dancing over the faces of the people pouring through the doors. "Counselor Dryden. I'm sorry she got killed."

Micah felt a jolt of regret as well, but he couldn't let that distract him now. "Answer the question, Snoop."

"What does it matter?"

"I don't understand you. One day, you're lying to me, the next, you're asking me for help. Could you not make up your mind?"

He shrugged and stared off into space. "I don't know you, white boy. I don't trust you. I don't know who you work for or why you do the things you do."

"Then why ask for my help if you couldn't trust me?"

Snoop winced and then tears spilled out of his wet eyes and down his cheeks. "You think I wanted to do any of this? You think I want to help Dos Cruces anymore?"

"Then why did you?"

"My son."

"Your son?"

For a long moment, Snoop didn't answer. He cried softly, pressing his palms together. "I was stupid to believe they would give him back to me, even if I did everything they wanted. He was ten years old. Ten years old. These are the kind of people I was trying to get away from. People who would snatch up and kill an innocent boy because of money. Because of some stupid vial in a container."

So much now made sense to Micah. Why Snoop had been unwilling to say before why he would make this deal. Micah had always assumed it was for money or out of a sense of loyalty, but it wasn't either of those things. Snoop had been motivated by something else entirely.

"Back when I first stole it," Snoop said, "things were different. Me and Dos Cruces were good. But things changed. They didn't trust me anymore. I had to protect myself and find a way that we could all walk away from this shit-storm alive. I never dreamed they would kidnap my boy to control me."

"When did they take him?" Micah said.

"A few days before I showed up at The Stone. Insurance to make sure I went through with the deal. It was the only way they could force my hand, since I wouldn't tell them the keycode. They stopped trying to get it out of me, just like the government did."

Snoop's lip trembled, and Micah waited for him to continue.

"They kept him someplace dark, quiet, in Oklahoma City. Some house in the northwest part of town. I kept thinking about him being there, alone, scared, waiting for someone to come rescue him. At that cluster-fuck yesterday, when it all went to hell, I tried to run. Tried to get him. When I showed up, he was already dead."

"That's why you ran off in the woods?"

"What was I supposed to do when a mountain of shit all collides at once? Can't be a coincidence that the Serbs and Dos Cruces all appeared there at the same time. That was the government, tipping the scales. They made it happen. They arranged that whole showdown. All I could do was cut my losses and try to… try to get my boy back and get him to Rosita so he could have some kind of life."

Micah didn't know what to say, so he said nothing. The government knew about it? Seemed unlikely. But so much was still unclear. Everything he knew about the situation, about Snoop, about Dos Cruces; he wasn't sure what to think of any of it now.

Snoop sniffled as the overhead speaker at the airport squawked. Future airplane passengers came and went, dragging rolling bags. People stared at their phones. Herded children like sheep.

"Who is Rosita?" Micah said.

"My sister. She adopted him when I started getting into trouble."

They fell silent as the airport bustled around them. Micah remembered the overheard conversation with this sister, him telling Rosita that he was going to fix it. He was going to get his son back.

Snoop wiped a runny nose on his sleeve. "You going to call the cops?"

"What will you do if I don't call them?"

Snoop looked back behind him at the security line into the terminal. "My flight leaves in three hours. I have a bed reserved at a halfway house in Ha Noi. It's a six-month program, and after that, I just want to live my life as a free man. No booze, no cartel, no US government."

Micah looked down at his phone, at the numbers 911 still entered into the keypad. He stared at the green *dial* button.

IN A WINDY and cold field outside of Hayes, Kansas, Frank Mueller sat on the hood of his rental car. He shivered. The sun hit the midpoint, and Frank's stomach rumbled. Surely, Hayes would have a good diner or two. You could always count on truck stop towns to supply that sort of thing. Lot lizards and hash browns. Frank had partaken in the hash browns on many occasions, but never the lot lizards. He'd arrested a few of them, though, back in his day.

As he waited, his thoughts drifted again to retirement, and if Micah would be ready to take over the business in a year or two. He'd proven himself quite capable as a skip tracer, even more so as a levelheaded, clever assistant. He'd make a fine bounty hunter.

If Micah even *wanted* to take over the business. Frank hadn't asked him yet.

The wind whipped along the plains, rustling fields of

decaying wheat in all directions. Frank did like the mountains of his adopted home in Colorado, but there was something about being able to see forever that appealed to him.

In another fifteen minutes, a Harley Davidson motorcycle roared into the field beside Frank's car. Once the rider had killed the engine, the silence that followed felt almost as loud.

Frank slid off the hood and greeted the man as he dismounted his bike. The man was wearing only a t-shirt, exposing his tattooed arms. Frank felt dwarfed next to this guy, and not just because of his height. The tattoos seemed to highlight the girth of his biceps, like tree trunks extending from his shoulders.

"Do you wear jackets?" Frank said.

"Sure, man, when it's cold."

Frank and his companion both grinned, then Frank retrieved the lockbox from the trunk of the car and passed it to the man. "Be careful with this."

The man examined the lockbox, eyeing the keypad on the front. "I know what to do."

"Are you sure you don't mind?"

"Not at all. I've been meaning to take a trip up north, and I just so happen to have a couple weeks with no contract work to speak of. Daughter is in Europe with her mom. Perfect timing, actually."

Frank slipped a piece of folded paper from his pocket and held it out. "This is the number to call once you're there."

"And they're expecting me?"

Frank nodded. "You don't anticipate problems at the border?"

"Oh no, man, don't sweat it. I've been across that border so many times, I know exactly what to do. Don't worry about me at all. But I gotta ask, why the secrecy? If this stuff is what you say it is, why can't you give it to the CDC or Homeland or somebody like that?"

Because Frank and Gavin had managed to keep it out of their hands, but he didn't want to say that. They'd been lucky that the SWAT agents the FBI had sent had no idea about the smallpox and weren't under the thumb of the NSA.

Frank paused to consider his words carefully. "My associate and I are having some trust issues with certain departments of government right now."

The man sucked his teeth, considering. "I get it. Believe me, I get it."

"This is a little off-topic, but, you work with a lot of big companies, right?"

"Sure, from time to time. The corporate stuff can be the most lucrative security consulting work. I mean, if you can handle dealing with the button-up types."

"You ever work with a company named Vanton Industries?"

The man screwed up his face, stared up at the wide open Kansas sky for a moment. "No, I can't say that I have."

"Ever heard of them, even?"

"I don't think so. Name doesn't ring a bell. Why?"

Frank shrugged. "It's probably nothing. Anyway, I'm sure you're ready to get on the road. And I still have a ways to go, too."

"No problem, Frank. You take care of yourself. I'll call you when I'm across the border."

They shook hands and Frank returned to his car, readying himself for the long drive back to Denver.

DAY 30

MICAH SAT AT his desk at Mueller Bail
Enforcement, staring at Frank's collection
of framed pictures on the wall. Frank, back
in his cop days, standing in front of a mountain of seized
cocaine bricks. Big, shit-eating grin on his face. Frank
had told the story of that bust so many times, Micah
knew it by heart.

Micah lifted the lid of his laptop and typed the name
of a certain Nevada billionaire into a Google search. He
clicked over to the *News* tab and scrolled down through
recent articles. One, in particular, caught his interest: the
billionaire had fled to Spain because of a government
investigation into some of his business practices. Assets
had been frozen. In-progress deals had been nullified.

Micah then opened a new browser tab and looked up
Kellen McBriar's Facebook page. Stared at the profile
picture, of Kellen and his wife and their two children, in

front of the Bellagio. The line of fountains behind them had been captured in mid-eruption, streaming jets of white into the air.

The smiles on their faces.

Micah tried not to think about how he could never let his brother know that he had been the one to prevent this terrible land deal from going through. That he would never be welcome in Kellen's house, and not only because Kellen believed Micah had died in the car crash after testifying against the Sinaloa. The last time they'd spoken, Micah had been Michael McBriar, a selfish drunk. A terrible brother.

Micah wouldn't get the chance to show his brother how much he had changed. And, he had to be okay with that. Had to be okay with knowing that staying far away from his family was the best thing he could do for them.

The bell on the door rang, and Micah smiled as his boss/AA sponsor walked through the door.

Micah checked an imaginary watch on his wrist. "Hey, bossman. Nice of you to show up for work. You're only... two days late."

"Sorry I didn't make it to the airport for our flight."

Frank wandered into the kitchen and poured himself a cup of coffee, then he hovered in the doorway, staring at Micah. "You get out of town okay?"

"Sure, Frank. I'm almost an adult so I can fly by myself."

Frank grinned. "I know you can. Don't give me a hard

time, kid. It was a hectic few days at the end there, so it's not too far out of school for me to ask after you."

"Fair enough, boss. Why your delay, though? Where've you been?"

Frank frowned, sighed through his nose. "I met with Layne."

Micah sat up straight. "Layne? Why?"

"I gave him a package to take to Canada."

"Gavin is okay with this?"

Frank nodded. "It was his idea, and that's all I'm going to say about it."

Micah waited to see if that was actually all Frank would say about it, and the old man kept his word. Micah had a good idea what the package was, and he trusted that if Frank didn't want to discuss it, then it was probably for everyone's protection.

They sat in silence for another minute. Frank sipped his coffee as Micah stared at the fractal screensaver blasting colors across his laptop screen.

"What about you?" Frank said. "Anything interesting happen to you on your way out of town?"

Micah shrugged and lowered his laptop's lid. "No, not that I can think of."

"You didn't happen to run into Snoop, did you? After he disappeared from Cornerstone, no one's been able to find him. He didn't show up at Tulsa International for his Vietnam flight."

Micah turned his palms up. "Not sure what to tell you. Maybe Dos Cruces got him, or maybe some other

Serbians, or who knows? I flew back here as soon as I could get a flight, and I've been waiting for you to show up."

Frank left the doorway and sat at his desk, then tilted his mug back as he stared across the divide between them. "Okay."

"Okay," Micah said. He didn't know if Frank believed him or not. And he didn't know if it mattered.

"Alright then," Frank said. "Let's see how much work we missed while we were gone."

With that, Frank put his coffee down and powered on his computer, and Micah waited for further instructions.

~

If you enjoyed this book, please click here to leave a review.

A MICAH REED
NOVEL

CATCH
AND
RELEASE

JIM HESKETT

Ready for more? Get the sequel at jimheskett.com/catch

A NOTE TO READERS

Ready for the sequel? Get it at
www.jimheskett.com/catch

If you started reading Micah Reed's adventure with this book, go back and take a peek at Airbag Scars. Micah's backstory will make a lot more sense, and you can get this full length novel FOR FREE at www.jimheskett.com

After college, I spent a few years working in the mental health field. Particularly, in drug and alcohol rehabilitation. It's an important field, and one fraught with complications and struggle. A thankless job, much of the time. As we've seen over the last few books, Micah has been changing as he stay sober. He's no longer always on the verge of a drink, and learning how to live life one day at a time. For this book, I liked the idea of him having to revisit those early days of sobriety by pretending to be someone fresh off a bender.

We now also have a wider picture of his family. He encountered his sister Magda in Nailgun Messiah, and now Micah has a chance to help his brother, even if indirectly. Plus, another opportunity to write a book set in small-town Oklahoma?

With that out of the way, thank you for reading my book!

Please consider leaving reviews on Goodreads and wherever else you purchased this book (links at jimheskett.com/stone). I know it's a pain, but you have no idea how much it will help the success of this book and my ability to write future books. That, sharing it on social media, and telling other people to read it.

Are you interested in joining a community of Jim Heskett fiction fans? Discuss the books with other people, including the author! Join for free at www.jimheskett.com/bookophile

I have a website where you can learn more about me and my other projects. Check me out at www.jimheskett.com and sign up for my reader group so you can stay informed on the latest news. You'll even get some freebies for signing up. You like free stuff, right?

For Bob: "I'm gonna recommend you read the anger book, cuz I'm guessing you got a lot of anger." Also, for Gloria, for showing me how far I had to go. For Bill, for listening to my first rambling attempt at an inventory. And for all the people who believed I would come back in a year to claim my cup.

Published by Royal Arch Books

Www.RoyalArchBooks.com
Please consider leaving a review once you have finished this book.
Want to know when the next book is coming out?
Join my mailing list to get updates and free stuff!

CHRONOLOGY

Micah Reed Chronology:

While the Micah Reed novels are essentially standalone stories, each one does build on some elements from previous books. To see the list of how each story fits on the overall timeline, visit jimheskett.com/timeline. If you want to read them in order, check out that link.

BOOKS BY JIM HESKETT

For a full list of all Jim Heskett's books, please visit
www.RoyalArchBooks.com

If you like thrillers, you'll want to take a gander at my
Whistleblower Trilogy. The first book, Wounded Animals,
follows the story of Tucker Candle, who meets a mysterious
stranger who warns him not to take a business trip. Candle
goes, however, and when he comes home, he discovers a dead
man in his bathroom and his wife is missing.

ABOUT THE AUTHOR

Jim Heskett was born in the wilds of Oklahoma, raised by a pack of wolves with a station wagon and a membership card to the local public swimming pool. Just like the man in the John Denver song, he moved to Colorado in the summer of his 27th year, and never looked back. Aside from an extended break traveling the world, he hasn't let the Flatirons mountains out of his sight.

He fell in love with writing at the age of fourteen with a copy of Stephen King's The Shining. Poetry became his first outlet for teen angst, then later some terrible screenplays, and eventually short and long fiction. In between, he worked a few careers that never quite tickled his creative toes, and hasn't ever forgotten about Stephen King. You can find him currently huddled over a laptop in an undisclosed location in Colorado, dreaming up ways to kill beloved characters.

He blogs at his own site and hosts the Indie Author

Answers Podcast. You can also scour the internet to find the occasional guest post or podcast appearance. A curated list of media appearances can be found at www.jimheskett.com/media

He believes the huckleberry is the king of berries and refuses to be persuaded in any other direction.

If you'd like to ask a question or just to say hi, stop by the About page and fill out the contact form.

For more info

www.jimheskett.com

Made in the USA
Lexington, KY
20 May 2019